"But you couldn't b... able to wake him. H..."

"No, Sami," he countered in a husky voice. "I'm right here."

She was so staggered to hear him use her nickname she clutched the crib railing with both hands. A small cry escaped her lips.

"You're Ric?" She shook her head, causing her hair to swish against her pale cheeks. "I—I can't believe this is happening. I—"

The room started to swim. The next thing Sami knew, she found herself on the bed, with the man who'd made her pregnant leaning over her. He sat next to her with his hands on either side of her head.

"Stay quiet for a minute. You've had another shock."

He spoke to her in the compassionate voice she remembered—exactly the way he'd done in the avalanche. With her eyes closed she could recall everything, and she was back there with him in spirit.

But the minute her eyelids fluttered open she saw a stranger staring down at her. In her psyche Sami knew he was Ric. But she couldn't credit that the striking, almost forbidding male who'd swept past her at the police station was the same Ric who'd once given her his passion and the will to live.

Dear Reader,

Born at the foot of the Wasatch mountains, my family has always enjoyed winter sports in our Rockies, which rise ten thousand feet. In my travels to Europe I've also enjoyed the winter ski areas in the Alps. Perhaps there's no place more breathtaking than Austria, where charming villages are tucked in at the base of the mountains, all covered in snow. Innsbruck is one of my favorite places.

When I read an article about an avalanche that swept through a street in one of those Austrian villages, killing five people, I shuddered. We're familiar with avalanches in our Utah mountains too. The tragedy stayed in my mind and wouldn't let me go until I'd written a novel about it.

When a man and a woman are trapped in a similar Austrian avalanche, their outcome beats the odds. I hope their story will thrill you.

Enjoy!

Rebecca Winters

REBECCA WINTERS

The Count's Christmas Baby

HARLEQUIN®
entertain, enrich, inspire™

Recycling programs
for this product may
not exist in your area.

ISBN-13: 978-0-373-17841-4

THE COUNT'S CHRISTMAS BABY

First North American Publication 2012

www.Harlequin.com

Printed in U.S.A.

Rebecca Winters, whose family of four children has now swelled to include five beautiful grandchildren, lives in Salt Lake City, Utah, in the land of the Rocky Mountains. With canyons and high alpine meadows full of wildflowers, she never runs out of places to explore. Along with her favorite vacation spots in Europe, they often end up as backgrounds for her romance novels. Writing is her passion, along with her family and church.

Rebecca loves to hear from readers. If you wish to email her, please visit her website: www.cleanromances.com.

Books by Rebecca Winters

Other titles by this author available in ebook format.

To my darling son John, a wonderful husband and father, who started skiing at four years of age and can ski like a champion. His experience and expertise both in the Utah and Colorado Rockies have helped me to add authenticity to the many mountain scenes in my books.

CHAPTER ONE

"Pat? It's me."

"Where are you?"

"At the Grand Savoia eating lunch in my room. You were right. It's a lovely place with every amenity. Thanks for arranging everything for me."

"You're welcome. How my gorgeous baby nephew holding up?"

"He's taking another nap right now, thank heaven. That's giving me time to pick up where I left off last evening."

"Couldn't you have phoned me before you went to bed to tell me how things were going? Your text saying you'd arrived in Genoa was hardly informative. I waited all day yesterday expecting to hear more from you."

"I'm sorry. After I reached the hotel, I began my search. But the telephone directory didn't have the listing I was looking for. When I realized I wouldn't find the answer there, I talked to the clerk at the front desk. He hooked me up with one of the chief phone operators who speaks English who was more than happy to help me."

"Why?"

In spite of the seriousness of the situation, her suspicious sister made her laugh. "It's a *she,* so you don't need to worry I'm being hit on. When I told her my dilemma, she couldn't have been nicer and tried to assist me any way she could. But by the time we got off the phone, I was too exhausted to call you."

"That's okay. So what's your plan now?"

"That operator suggested I should call the police station. She gave me the number for the traveler's assistance department. She said there'll be someone on duty who speaks English. They're used to getting calls from foreigners either stranded or in trouble and will help me. I'm going to do that as soon as I hang up from you."

"And what if you still don't have success?"

"Then I'll fly home in the morning as planned and never think about it again."

"I'm going to hold you to that. To be frank, I hope you've come to a dead end. Sometimes it's better not to know what you don't know. It could come back to bite you."

"What do you mean?"

"Just what I said. You might be walking into something you wish you could have avoided. Not all people are as nice and good as you are, Sami. I don't want to see you hurt."

"You're not by any chance having one of your premonitions, are you?"

"No, but I can't help my misgivings." Pat sounded convinced Sami had come to Italy on a fool's errand. Maybe she had.

"Tell you what. If he's not in Genoa, then I'll be on the next plane home."

"I'm going to hold you to that. Forgive me if I don't wish you luck. Before you go to bed tonight, call me. I don't care what time it is. Okay?"

"Okay. Love you."

"Love you, too."

Sami hung up, wondering if her sister was right. Maybe she shouldn't be searching for the grandfather of her baby. If she did find him, he might be so shocked to find out he was a grandfather, it could upset his world and make him ill. Possibly their meeting could turn so ugly, she'd wish she'd never left home.

That's what worried Pat.

If Sami were being honest, it worried her, too. But as long as she'd come this far, she might as well go all the way. Then maybe she could end this chapter of her life and move on.

She looked at the number she'd written down on her pad and made the phone call. The man who answered switched to English after she said hello. "Yes?"

His peremptory response took her back. "Is this the traveler's assistance department?"

"Yes—"

"I wonder if you could help me."

"What is it you want?"

Whoa. "I'm trying to find a man named Alberto Degenoli who's supposed to be living in Genoa, but he's not listed in the city phone directory. I've come from the United States looking for him. I was hoping y—"

But she stopped talking because the man, whom she'd thought was listening, was suddenly talking to another man in rapid Italian. Soon there was a third voice. Their conversation went on for at least a minute before the first man said, "Please spell the name for me."

When she did his bidding, more unintelligible Italian followed in the background. Finally, "You come to the station and ask for Chief Coretti."

Chief?

"You mean now?"

"Of course." The line went dead.

She blinked at his bizarre phone manners, but at least he hadn't turned her away. That had to account for something.

Next she phoned the front desk and asked them to send up the hotel's childminder. Sami had interviewed the qualified nurse yesterday and felt good about her. While she waited for her to come, she refreshed her makeup and slipped on her suit jacket.

Only four people knew the private cell phone number of Count Alberto Enrico Degenoli. When the phone rang, Ric assumed it was his fiancée, Eliana, calling again to dissuade him from leaving on a business trip in a few minutes. She was her father's puppet after all.

Now that Ric was about to become the son-in-law of one of the wealthiest industrialists in Italy, her father expected to control every portion of Ric's life, too. But Ric had crucial private business on Cyprus no one knew about, and it had to be transacted before the wedding.

Love had no part of this marriage and Eliana knew it. The coming nuptials were all about money. However, once they exchanged vows, he planned to do his part to make the marriage work. But until Christmas Eve, his time and business were his own concern and his future father-in-law couldn't do anything to stop him.

When he glanced away from his office computer screen long enough to check the caller ID, he discovered it was his private secretary phoning from the palazzo.

He clicked on. "Mario?"

"Forgive the interruption, Excellency." The older man had been in the service of the Degenoli family as private secretary for thirty-five years. But he was old-fashioned and insisted on being more formal with Ric now that Ric held the title. "Chief of Police Coretti just called the palace requesting to speak to you. He says it's extremely urgent, but refused to tell me the details. You're to call him back on his private line."

That would have irked Mario, who'd been privy to virtually everything in Ric's life. In all honesty, the chief's secrecy alarmed even Ric, whose concern over the reason for the call could touch on more tragedy and sorrow for their family. They'd had enough for several lifetimes.

"Give me the number."

After writing it down, he thanked Mario, then clicked off and made the call. "Signor Coretti? It's Enrico Degenoli. What can I do for you?"

He hadn't talked to the chief since the funeral for his father, who'd died in an avalanche in January. The chief had been among the dignitaries in Genoa who'd met the plane carrying his father's body. The memories of what had happened that weekend in Austria would always haunt Ric and had changed the course of his life.

"Forgive me for interrupting you, but there's a very attractive American woman in my office just in from the States who's looking for an Alberto Degenoli from Genoa."

At first his heart leaped at the news, then as quickly fizzled. If this American woman had been looking for him, she would have told the police chief she was looking for a man named Ric Degenoli.

Ric and his father bore the same names, but his father had gone by Alberto, and Ric went by Enrico. Only his siblings ever called him Ric. *And the woman who'd been caught with him in the avalanche.*

"Does she know my father died?"

"If she does, she has said nothing. To be frank, it's my opinion she's here on a fishing expedition, *if* you know what I mean." He cleared his throat. "She's hoping I can find him for her because she says it's a matter of life and death," he added in a quiet voice.

What?

"Since she's being suspiciously secretive, I thought I should let you know before I told her anything."

The intimation that this could be something of a delicate nature alarmed Ric in a brand-new way. He shot out of his leather chair in reaction. Up to now he'd done everything possible to protect his family from scandal.

Unfortunately he hadn't been able to control his father's past actions. No matter that Ric was a Degenoli, he and his father had differed in such fundamental ways, including the looks he'd inherited from his mother, that the average person wouldn't have known they were father and son.

One of Ric's greatest fears was that his father's weakness for women would catch up with him in ways he didn't want to think about. With his own marriage coming up on New Year's Day, it was imperative nothing go wrong at this late date. Too much was riding on it.

His father had been dead less than a year. It wasn't a secret he'd been with several women since Ric's mother's sudden and unexpected death from pneumonia sixteen months ago. He recalled his mother once confiding to him that even if his father were penniless, he would always be attractive to women and she had overlooked his wandering eye.

Ric couldn't be that generous. If the woman in Coretti's office thought she could blackmail their family or insist she had some claim on his deceased father's legacy, then she hadn't met Ric and was deluding herself. "What's her name?"

"Christine Argyle."

The name meant nothing to him. "Is she married? Single?"

"I don't know. Her passport didn't indicate one way or the other, but she wasn't wearing a ring. She called the traveler's aid department and they turned it over to me. At first I thought this must be some sort of outlandish prank, but she's not backing down. Since this is about your father, I thought I'd better phone you and learn your wishes before I tell her I can't help her and order her off the premises."

"Thank you for handling this with diplomacy," Ric said in a level voice, but his anger boiled beneath the surface. To go straight to Genoa's chief of police to get his attention was a clever tactic on her part. She wouldn't have taken that kind of a risk unless she thought she had something on Ric's father that the family wouldn't like made public. *How convenient and predictable.*

She'd probably met Alberto at a business party last fall when he'd decided he didn't want to be in mourning any longer. More often than not those dinners involved private gambling parties. Many of them were hosted for foreign VIPs on board one of the yachts anchored in the harbor where the police had no jurisdiction.

There'd be plenty of available women, including American starlets, to please every appetite. But it would be catastrophic if this last fling of his father's was the one that couldn't be hushed up and resulted in embarrassing the family morally and financially.

Not if Ric could help it!

Anything leaked to the press now could affect Ric's future plans in ways he didn't even want to think about. He saw red. Before the wedding, the negotiations in Cyprus *had* to go through as planned to safeguard his deceased mother's assets so Eliana's father couldn't get his hands on them. Ric refused to let anything get in the way.

"*Per favore*—keep her in your office until I get there. Don't use my title in front of her. Simply introduce me as Signor Alberto Degenoli and I'll go from there." This

woman wouldn't have gotten involved with his father if
he hadn't had a title, but Ric intended to play along with
her ruse until he'd exposed her for a grasping opportunist.

"Understood. She went out for a while, but she'll be
calling me in a few minutes. If you're coming now, I'll
let her know you're on your way."

His thoughts were reeling. "Say nothing about this
to anyone."

"Surely you don't question my loyalty to the House
of Degenoli?"

"No," Ric muttered, furrowing his hair absently with
his fingers. He stared blindly out the window of the
Degenoli Shipping Lines office. For well on 150 years it
had overlooked the port of Genoa, Italy's most important
port city. "Forgive me, but when it comes to my family..."

"I understand. You know you can rely on my discre-
tion."

"Grazie." Ric's voice grated before he hung up.

Whatever was going on, Ric didn't want wind of this
to reach his siblings. Claudia and Vito lived with enough
pain and didn't need to take on more, especially with
Christmas only a week away. It was absolutely essential
this be kept secret.

After he told his driver to meet him in the side alley,
he rang security to follow them and left the office with
his bodyguards. He needed to take care of this matter
now, before he left for the airport.

For the second time today, Sami paid the taxi driver and
got out in front of the main police station in Genoa with

trepidation. The police chief had told her one of his staff had found the number of the man she was looking for and had contacted him.

It was a miracle! She couldn't have done it without the phone operator's help. After searching for Alberto Degenoli without success, she'd almost given up hope.

No telling what would happen at this meeting, but she had to go through with it for her baby's sake. His existence would come as a total surprise to Mr. Degenoli, but her son deserved to know about his father's side of the family.

Of course, the baby was too little to know anything yet. It was up to Sami to introduce them and lay a foundation for the future, *if* Mr. Degenoli wanted a relationship. If not, then she'd go back to Reno and raise him without feeling any attendant guilt that she hadn't done all she could do to unite them.

Once through the doors, she realized it was just as busy at four o'clock as it had been earlier. Besides people and staff, it was filled with cigarette smoke, irritating her eyes and nose. The nativity scene set up on a table in the foyer reminded her how close it was to Christmas and she'd done nothing to get ready for it yet. But she'd had something much more important on her mind before leaving Reno than the upcoming holidays.

Having been in the building earlier, she knew where to go. She'd just started to make her way down the hall when a man strode swiftly past her and rounded a corner at the end. He was a tall male, elegantly dressed in a tan suit and tie. Maybe he was in his mid-thirties. For want of a better word, he left an impression of power and importance that appeared unconscious and seemed to come as naturally to him as breathing.

Sami passed several men and policemen who eyed her in masculine appreciation before she turned the corner and entered the reception area of the police chief's office. With the exception of the uniformed male receptionist she'd met before, the room was empty. Where had the other man gone?

After she sat down, the receptionist picked up the phone, presumably to let the chief know she'd arrived. Once he'd hung up, he told her she could go in. After removing a few blond hairs from the sleeve of her navy blazer, Sami thanked him and opened the door to the inner office.

To her shock, the stranger who'd passed her in the hall moments ago was standing near the chief's desk talking to him. Obviously the chief of police was busy, so she didn't understand why his secretary had told her she could go in.

At a glance she took in the other man's lean, powerful physique. Her gaze quickly traveled to the lines of experience etched around his eyes and mouth. Maybe she was mistaken, but beneath his black brows, those dark eyes pierced hers with hostility after he'd turned in her direction. That wasn't a reaction she was used to receiving from the opposite sex.

Of medium height, she had to look up to him. His unique male beauty fascinated her, especially his widow's peak formed by hair black as midnight. Swept back like that, it brought his Mediterranean features and gorgeous olive skin into prominence.

The chief spoke in heavily accented English, drawing her attention away from the stranger. "Signorina, may I present Signor Alberto Degenoli."

Sami's spirits plunged. *This isn't the man I'm looking for.* But perhaps he is a relative? "How do you do?" she murmured, shaking the hand of the striking Italian male who'd extended his. He had a strong, firm grip, like the man himself.

"How do *you* do, Signorina?" His polished English was impeccable with barely a whisper of accent. But it was the depth of his voice that sent a curious shiver through her body, recalling an echo from the past. Maybe she was mistaken, but she thought she'd heard that voice before.

But that was crazy. They'd never met.

"You've gone pale, Signorina. Are you all right?"

"Yes—" Sami gripped the back of the nearest chair. "I-it's just that you're not the person I'm looking for and I'm disappointed," she stammered before gazing at him again. "You have his name, but you're…too young. Obviously there's more than one Alberto Degenoli living in Genoa."

He shook his head. "No. There's only one."

"You mean *you?*"

"That's right."

"Perhaps instead of Genova, you meant Geneva in Switzerland, Signorina," the chief inserted. "Many

Americans become confused by the two similar spellings."

She frowned. "Possibly I misunderstood. Mr. Degenoli's in shipping."

"So are others on Lake Geneva."

"But he's Italian."

"Thousands of Italians live in Switzerland."

"Yes. I know." Maybe because of the differences in pronunciation, she'd gotten the name of the city wrong. How odd. All this time... "Thank you for the suggestion." She looked at Mr. Degenoli. "I'm so sorry you've made this trip to the police station for nothing. I've put both of you out. Please forgive me."

"Perhaps if you gave me a clearer description of him?"

"Well, he'd probably be in his sixties. I'm not sure. I feel terrible about this. Thank you for coming here on such short notice." She glanced at Chief Coretti. "Please excuse me for taking up your time. You've been very kind. I'll leave now so you can get on with your work."

At her comment, he squinted at her. "You sounded desperate when you came to me, Signorina. Therefore I will leave you to get better acquainted with this gentleman you've inconvenienced, and the two of you can discuss...business."

Business? "What on earth do you mean?"

"Surely you're not that naive?" the chief replied.

Upset by the distasteful insinuation, she felt heat rush to her cheeks. "You've evidently questioned my motives, but whatever you're thinking, you'd be wrong—" she blurted.

At this point she felt oddly reluctant to be left alone with the intimidating stranger studying her with relentless scrutiny. "I haven't found the person I'm looking for, so there's no point in this going any further. I truly am sorry to have caused either of you any inconvenience."

Chief Coretti gave her a nasty smile. "What is going on, Signorina? You said it was a matter of life and death."

"It is." She hated the tremor in her voice.

He threw up his hands. "So explain!"

"I know I've been secretive, but I'm trying to make this inquiry as discreetly as possible to protect all concerned. When my other searches failed yesterday, I came to you for answers and hoped nobody would get hurt in the process. But the fact remains I'm looking for an older gentleman. I suppose he could even be in his early seventies."

Time seemed suspended as Mr. Degenoli swallowed her up with those jet-black eyes of his. "Signor Coretti—if you'd be so kind as to leave us alone for a moment."

"Of course."

After he left, the room grew silent as a tomb except for the thudding of her heart. It wouldn't surprise her if the stranger could hear it.

His lips twisted unpleasantly before he moved closer. "You've been secretive long enough. I'd like to see your passport." Sami had the strongest conviction he was curious about her, too. At this point she knew she'd heard his voice before. But where? When she'd come to Europe a year ago, she hadn't visited Italy.

While she rummaged in her purse, her mind was

searching to remember. He stood there waiting, larger than life with an air of authority much more commanding than any police chief's. She handed the passport to him. After he read the information, he gave it back.

"I've never heard of you." His eyes glittered with barely suppressed anger. "The Alberto Degenoli I believe you're looking for is no longer alive, but I think you already knew that. How well did you know him?" he demanded.

Ah. Now she understood the police chief's earlier remark about "business." Both men assumed she'd been involved with the man she was looking for. Sami lifted her head. "I didn't know him at all. In fact I never met him, but I'd h-hoped to," she stammered. Sadness overwhelmed her to realize she'd come to Italy for nothing.

"What did this man mean to you?"

Wouldn't he just love to know, but he'd be so wrong! She took a fortifying breath. "Since he's dead…nothing."

"How did you hear of him?"

Sami had heard of him through his son, but he was dead, too. If this man was the only living Degenoli in Genoa, then what the chief of police had said was probably true. She should fly to Geneva to start her search there before flying home.

"It no longer matters." She tried to swallow, but the sudden swelling in her throat made it difficult. "Forgive me for bothering you." She spun around and made a quick exit.

As she flew down the hall to the entrance of the police station, she suddenly realized what had been bothering her. The man she'd just left had the same kind of voice as her baby's deceased father. That's why it had sounded so familiar and disturbing…except for one thing.

This man didn't have that tender, caring quality in his voice. His tone and manner had been borderline accusatory. Her body gave a shudder before she stepped into the first taxi in the line-up in front of the building.

Ric had caught only a glimpse of tear-filled green eyes before she dashed from Coretti's office. Could there be two American women in existence who sounded that identical? He supposed the coincidence was possible, since he'd never seen this woman in his life.

For months he'd looked for the woman he'd been trapped in the snow with, hoping she would come looking for him, but by summer he'd decided she must have died in that avalanche.

He closed his eyes for a moment, remembering the way this woman's husky voice had trembled. Much as he hated to admit it, a part of him had felt her emotion was genuine. The classic features of her pale blond beauty, so different from his own countrywomen, already bothered him in ways he was reluctant to admit.

But great as her acting had been, Ric was convinced Signorina Argyle had lied to him, or at least hadn't told him the whole truth. Whatever her secret, he was determined to find it out.

Running on pure adrenaline at this point, he buzzed Carlo, his head of security, and told him to follow the twenty-six-year-old blonde American woman leaving the police station. When she reached her destination, he wanted to know exactly where she went from there, so he could arrange a private meeting.

Now hadn't been the time to stop her. The conversation he intended to have with her needed to be someplace where they could be strictly alone with no chance of anyone else walking in on them.

With his visit to the chief's office accomplished, he went out to the limo. Within a few minutes he learned she was booked in at the Grand Savoia—one of the best, if not *the* best hotel in Genoa. It was expensive any time, but especially over the holidays. He told the driver to take him there. Carlo indicated Ric would find her on the third floor, to the right of the elevator, four doors down on the left.

Before long he alighted from the limo and entered the hotel. Deciding to take her by surprise, he dispensed with the idea of phoning her and took the stairs two at a time to her floor. When he reached her door, he knocked loudly enough for her to hear.

"Signorina Argyle? It's Signor Degenoli. We need to talk." He got no response, so he decided to try a different tactic. "Why were you trying to find Alberto? I would like to help you if you'd let me."

Carlo had told him she'd gone into her room and hadn't come out again, but she might be showering. He gave her another minute, then knocked again. "Signorina?"

A few seconds later the door opened as wide as the little chain would allow. He saw those green eyes lifted to him in consternation, but they were red-rimmed. By the look of it, she'd been crying. That much was genuine.

The champagne-gold of her collar-length hair gleamed in the hall light. She'd discarded her jacket. From the little he could see, a curvaceous figure was revealed beneath the silky white blouse she'd tucked in at the waist of her navy skirt. Every inch of her face and body appealed strongly to him.

"I didn't realize the police chief had had me followed." The natural shape of her mouth had a voluptuous flare he'd noticed back at the station. But right now it was drawn tight. She hugged the door, as if she didn't trust him not to break in on her.

Ric lounged against the wall. "Don't blame him. I asked one of my men to keep an eye on you until I could catch up with you."

"*Your* men?"

"My bodyguards. If you'll invite me inside, I'll be happy to explain."

A delicate frown marred her features. "I'm sorry, Mr. Degenoli, but as I said at the station, there's nothing more to discuss and I have other plans."

"As do I." He was already late leaving for Cyprus. "But we have unfinished business," he rapped out. To his disgust, he wondered what her exact plans were. Deep inside, his gut twisted to think that he could be this intensely attracted to a stranger. His interest in her made no sense, but the sound of her voice and the way she talked still played with his senses.

A sound of exasperation escaped her lips. "Please believe me when I tell you how badly I feel that you were called into the police station for nothing. If you'd like me to pay you for the inconvenience, I could give you fifty dollars to cover the gas money. It's all I can spare."

If that were true, then she'd chosen too expensive a hotel to stay in. "I don't want your money. To be frank, I knew you were upset when you left the station." He cocked his head. "I can tell you've been crying. Now that we don't have Chief Coretti for an audience, you can speak freely with me."

"I probably could, but there'd be no point." She wiped her eyes with the back of her hands. "I've come to the end of my search. I have to say goodbye now."

There was no question in his mind she was holding back something vital. He put his foot in the door so she couldn't close it. "Not until I get more answers. For one thing—" He only got that far because he heard a baby fussing. The sounds came from the other side of the door. *I knew it!*

"Not so fast." Ric put his weight against the door so she couldn't shut it on him. "Whose baby is it?"

"Mine."

"And Alberto's?" With his mind firing, all Ric could think was that his father had made love to this woman and she'd come to present him with the fruit of that union, but it was too late.

"No—" she cried.

"Then prove it to me."

CHAPTER TWO

IN HER mind Sami could hear Pat's dire warning, but she hadn't heeded it.

This situation had hit rock bottom and was exactly what she'd hoped to avoid, but this man wouldn't let it go and had followed her to the hotel. Since she'd started this, she decided that if she didn't want to deal with Chief Coretti again, she'd better let him in.

After undoing the chain, she hurried across the room to the crib. Once she'd picked up the baby, she cuddled him against her shoulder in a protective gesture. Kissing him, she said, "You heard noises and they frightened you, didn't they, sweetheart? Don't worry. It's okay." She flicked Mr. Degenoli a curious glance. "Our visitor will be leaving soon."

The arresting-looking Italian had already come inside the room and locked the door behind him. She shivered a little as he drew closer to look at her baby.

Sami decided *this* Mr. Degenoli *had* to be a relative of her baby's father. That's why his voice sounded so familiar to her. Back at the station he'd been as cagey as she'd tried to be in her effort to protect people and reputations, even to the extent of possibly lying about his name, but with both father and son dead, there was no worry now. The only thing to do was answer his questions, then go home to Reno in the morning.

"Excuse me while I change him." Reaching for a towel, she spread it on top of the bed and put the baby down.

"Where did you leave him while you were at the police station?"

Sami undid the baby's stretchy blue suit. "Here, of course. Don't you know the last place for a baby was that smoke-filled building? This hotel happens to have an outstanding child-minding service." Sami's sister had made the reservation for her. "That's the reason I booked in here. They sent a qualified nurse to watch over him while I went to the police station."

He didn't look as if he believed her. "I didn't kidnap him. If you're so skeptical, call the front desk and ask them yourself. They'll verify who I am."

At this point his eyes were riveted on the baby. "How old is he?"

Sami used the baby wipes and discarded everything in a plastic bag. After powdering him, she slipped him into a fresh diaper. "Two months, but that information wouldn't have any relevance for you. I couldn't bring him to Genoa to meet his grandfather before now."

"Grandfather—"

"Yes. Why do you seem so shocked? Most children have them. I'm heartbroken that my son is never going to know him or…his father." Her voice faltered.

She kissed the soft baby hair that was dark and too

beautiful for a boy. His handsome face was all flushed, but he stopped crying long enough to notice the intruder who was thoroughly inspecting him.

After fastening the snaps on the stretchy suit, she wrapped him in his quilt and picked him up to snuggle him. "I think you're ready for your dinner, young man." She walked over to the dresser for a fresh bottle of ready-mixed formula and sat down on a chair to feed him.

"Your voice sounds familiar to me, Signorina."

So she wasn't the only one imagining their connection. "Yours does to me, too. Strange, isn't it, when I know we've never met?"

His dark brows furrowed. "More than strange. Were you in Europe on holiday recently?"

"Not for close to a year, but I've traveled to Europe before."

"I'd like to see your passport again."

"Let me feed my son first, then I'll get it for you."

He was a good little eater, but he'd been awakened before his nap had been over and was ready to go back to sleep. She burped him, then put him back in the crib and covered him with the quilt.

Aware of Mr. Degenoli's eyes watching her every move, she walked over to the dresser and pulled the passport from her purse. "In case you were wondering, I applied for this passport several years before my baby was born."

Her visitor took it from her and studied the pages with the various entry stamps. "This last one dated in January says you visited Austria—"

"Yes."

"*Where* in Austria?" The inflexible male sounded in deadly earnest.

"Innsbruck."

At the mention of it, his complexion took on a definite pallor. "Why that town?"

"Because my sister and her husband own a travel agency, and I was checking out some hotels for them there and in the surrounding areas. They're always looking for new places to book their clients into."

Mr. Degenoli appeared so shaken, she decided to end their inane question-and-answer session. Without hesitation she reached for her purse and pulled out a brown envelope. "Here—" Sami handed it to him. "I brought this to show my baby's grandfather. It will explain everything."

He eyed her suspiciously before he opened it and pulled out the birth certificate.

"As you can see there, I named my baby Ric, after his daddy. Ric Argyle Degenoli. You see, b-both Ric and his father, Alberto, were caught up in the same avalanche I was buried in last January." Her voice faltered. "I assume Alberto was a relative of yours. Maybe your uncle?"

Her uninvited guest didn't make a sound. It led her to believe he was finally listening to her. "I'd just stopped in one of the hotels for a minute to check it out and get a hot drink in the dining room. As I was about to go outside again to do a little sightseeing, the avalanche swept through the three-story hotel like a supersonic freight train.

"Ric and I were entombed for several hours. I knew he'd died before I lost total consciousness, but until you told me at the police station, I didn't realize Alberto had been killed, too.

"After I woke up in a clinic, I assumed Ric's father had survived, because only one male victim named Degenoli was listed among the fatalities. That was Ric, of course. His father must have died later from his injuries, after the list was put out."

Sami couldn't stop the tears from spurting. "It was a nightmarish time. My sister came to Innsbruck to get me and fly home with me. I didn't realize until six weeks later that I was pregnant. At that point I determined that one day I'd look up Alberto and let him know he had a grandchild. But as you've let me know, this trip was in vain."

The man listening to her story had gone eerily quiet.

"My sister calls my son Ricky, but I love the Italian version. I named him after his heroic father to honor him."

"Heroic?" he questioned in a gravelly voice.

"Yes. One day when Ric is old enough, I'll tell him how courageous his father was."

"In what way?"

"You would have to have been there to understand. Ric was an amazing man. After the snow buried us, he kept me from losing my mind. You see, I suffer from claustrophobia. You can't imagine what being trapped did to me. I wouldn't be alive if it hadn't been for him.

"We were total strangers sealed in a black tomb together. We heard each other moan, but had no idea what the other one looked like. I know I was on the verge of a heart attack when he started talking to me and urged me to relax, because he believed we'd get out of there if we didn't panic. He pointed out that by some miracle, we were trapped by beams that kept the whole weight from falling on us, providing us a pocket of air and room to wiggle.

"At first I thought I was dead and that he was an angel the way he took care of me and never let me panic. But when he reached for me and held me in his arms, promising me we'd be all right, I knew he was mortal.

"His only thought was to protect me. At first his kisses on my cheek held back my terror. I returned them, needing his comfort while we lay there slowly suffocating. We talked a little. He told me he'd just come from a wedding with his father, Alberto. I explained I was on a trip, but we didn't go into details.

"As time went on and no help came, we realized we were going to die. At that point we drew warmth and comfort from each other's bodies." She took a fortifying breath. "We made love. It happened so naturally, it was like a dream. Then I heard a shifting sound. The next thing I knew a piece of wood had pierced his forehead."

A sob caught in her throat. "It knocked him unconscious and his warm blood spilled over both of us. I couldn't get a pulse and knew he was gone. When I woke up in a clinic, the last thing I remembered was that he'd died in my arms.

"We'd been literally tossed together with the broken

walls and furniture in the darkness of a catastrophic avalanche that hit the hotel. But for the time we were together, hanging on to life because we knew they were our last moments on this earth, I felt closer to him than to anyone I've ever known.

"When I look at my adorable Ric, I know I'm seeing his father. My only hope now is to raise him to measure up to the great man who gave him life. I know he was a great man because he was so selfless in the face of terror. He never once thought of himself, only of me. So now I hope that explanation answers your questions, Mr. Degenoli."

She stared at the tall figure still standing there. His face had gone ashen. The birth certificate had fallen to the floor. How odd he'd left it there...

"If you still don't believe me, then I don't know what more I can say to convince you. Maybe now you'd answer a question for me. Was Alberto your uncle?"

"No," he answered in a voice as deep as a cavern. "He was my father."

"Chief Coretti introduced you as Alberto, but that really isn't your name, is it? He did it to protect you. I can understand that."

He moved closer to her. "Let me explain this another way. My father was christened Alberto Enrico Degenoli, and was called Alberto. I was also christened Alberto Enrico Degenoli, but I go by Enrico. However my immediate family calls me...Ric."

As Sami stared at him, the world tilted.

"But you *couldn't* be that Ric. I wasn't able to waken him. He died in my arms—"

"No, Sami," he countered in a husky voice. "I'm right here."

She was so staggered to hear him use her nickname, she clutched the crib railing with both hands. A small cry escaped her lips. "*You're* Ric?" She shook her head, causing her hair to swish against her pale cheeks. "I—I can't believe this is happening. I—"

The room started to swim. The next thing Sami knew, she found herself on the bed with the man who'd made her pregnant leaning over her. He sat next to her with his hands on either side of her head. "Stay quiet for a minute. You've had another shock."

He spoke to her in the compassionate voice she remembered—exactly the way he'd done in the avalanche. With her eyes closed, she could recall everything and was back there with him in spirit.

But the minute her eyelids fluttered open, she saw a stranger staring down at her. In her psyche Sami knew he was Ric. But she couldn't credit that the striking, almost forbidding male who'd swept past her at the police station was the same Ric who'd once given her his passion and the will to live.

Sami's hair spilled onto Ric's fingers. If he closed his eyes, he could recall the same silky mane he'd played with in the darkness. The strands had been as fragrant as every part of her face and body. It was the same now, but at the time he'd had no idea its coloring resembled spun gossamer.

Still noticing her pallor, he got up from the bed to get her a cup of water. When he returned from the bathroom, she sat up. He handed it to her and she drank thirstily. "Thank you," she whispered in a tremulous voice before lying back again like a spent flower.

Ric put the empty cup on the side table, then sank down next to her once more. "Our survival was a miracle," he began.

"Yes. I'm still trying to deal with the fact that you didn't die and are here where I can see you."

She wasn't the only one. "When we were trapped together, I would have sold my soul to know what you looked like," he confessed emotionally. "Feeling you told me that you were a lovely woman, but I must admit that no dreams I've had of you could measure up to your living reality."

Like someone shell-shocked, she lifted one of her hands to his face in wonder. She traced his features, bringing back memories he would never forget. "Ric—" Her fingers traveled over his lips. "Maybe I'm hallucinating again."

He kissed the palm of her hand. "It was never an hallucination. We were mortal then and now."

Tears trickled out of the corners of her eyes, eyes that were alive like the green of a tropical rain forest. "When I thought you were dead, I wanted to die. While you were still breathing, I could hold on. But after that beam hit you and I couldn't get a response, it was the end of my world."

Ric heard the same pain in her voice he'd carried around for months afterward. He studied her facial features, overlaying his memories of her through eyes that could see the throb at the base of her slender throat. Tears trembled on the ends of long dark lashes so unusual on a blonde.

She kept looking at him with incredulity. "I feel just like I did after the avalanche struck. Maybe I'm hallucinating and none of this is real, but it *has* to be real because I'm touching you and it's your voice. You're actual flesh and blood instead of the stuff of my dreams."

"You were the flesh and blood I clung to while we were entombed," he confessed. "You saved my sanity, too, Sami. Like you, I felt I was in this amazing dream. When we made love, I remember thinking that if it was a dream, I never wanted to wake up from that part of it. Everything about our experience had a surreal quality."

Sami wiped the tears off her face. "I know. Until I found out I was pregnant, there were times when I thought I'd made it all up." She stared at him. "What happened to you after you were rescued?"

He grasped her hand. "I was told that another few minutes and the medics wouldn't have been able to revive me. I knew nothing until I woke up in a hospital in Genoa. I was in a coma for two days. When I came out of it, I was surrounded by my family. My first request of the doctor was to find out if you were one of the victims.

"He came back with the message that you must still

be alive because there was no name of Sami or anything close to it on the list of fatalities. After hearing that news, I determined to go after you once I got better. After our family held funeral services for my father, then I started looking for you."

"I can't believe it."

"Why are you so surprised? What we'd shared together was something so unique, I'll never forget. But when your name didn't show up on any established tour-group lists in the area, I had to look further afield. I remembered you'd told me you were from Oakland, California. That's all I had to go on. I put my people on it while we searched for you for several months."

"Oh, Ric—" she cried softly before sliding off the other side of the bed to come around.

He got to his feet. "You were my first priority, but you weren't listed in the Oakland phone directory. No flights leaving Austria for the States with your name. No planes arriving in Oakland or San Francisco had a name that could be traced to you. It was as if you'd disappeared off the face of the earth."

"That's because you didn't know my real name," she cried out in dismay. "I was nicknamed Sami because my father's name was Samuel. After my parents died, my grandparents took over raising me and my sister, and my grandfather said I reminded him so much of his son he started calling me Sami, and it stuck."

"I thought it had to be short for Samantha, but your passport says otherwise."

"That's what everyone assumes who doesn't know

me. To think you searched all that time for the wrong name. I can't bear it."

He couldn't either, considering the promise he'd made to his father when they'd gone to Austria for an important family wedding. Ric had done everything humanly possible to find her. When he'd exhausted every avenue to no avail, he'd got on with his life and eventually fulfilled that promise.

"It's true I was born and raised in Oakland," she went on to explain, "but after I went back to college, I started to feel ill and went to a doctor. When he told me I was pregnant, I couldn't believe it. My sister, Pat, insisted I move to Reno, Nevada, to be with her and her husband. Their travel agency is growing all the time. They're the ones who gave me a working vacation during my break from college."

Nevada... The avalanche had changed both their lives in ways Ric was only beginning to understand. "Were you ill the whole pregnancy?"

"No. After the morning sickness passed, I didn't have other problems. Since Pat's my only family and I wanted to be close to her and their children, I moved to Reno and started classes there. Without my legal name, no wonder you couldn't trace me."

He rubbed his chest absently while he was digesting everything.

Her anxious gaze fastened on him. 'Do you have any ill effects from your head wound?"

"Only the occasional headache," he answered, touched by her concern.

"I'm so glad it isn't worse. That was the most terrifying moment." Her voice shook.

"Thankfully, I don't remember."

"I don't like to think about it. Throughout my pregnancy I decided that after Ric was born and I'd had my six-weeks checkup, I'd take him to Genoa and look up his grandfather. My own parents had already died, and I thought it would be wonderful if Ric grew up knowing he had at least one grandparent who was still alive." She hugged her arms to her waist. "How tragic you lost your father."

"Yes," he whispered, but right now everything else seemed very far removed.

"I thought about him all the time," she said. "Naturally I feared how he would take the news. It might have been the worst thing he could hear, but I hoped it might comfort him a little to know you weren't alone when you died."

Ric's breath caught. "*Ringrazio il cielo* you looked for him! Otherwise I would know nothing! Be assured my father would have wanted to be a grandfather to our son." *Once he'd gotten over the shock of learning the circumstances of his grandson's conception.* Ric was still having trouble taking it all in.

She bit her lip. "I didn't know the right thing to do. That's the reason why I was so secretive with the police chief." Ric warmed to her for her desire to be discreet. "I didn't want to embarrass your father or cause him pain in front of anyone else. I really thought if I could find him, he'd refuse to believe me and that would be the end of it. But for the baby's sake, I felt I had to try.

"When the police chief suggested maybe I had the wrong city, I didn't know what to believe. I thought you'd told me you were from Genoa. The thought of flying to Geneva and starting another search sounded overwhelming, but I was prepared to do it for your son's sake. Oh, Ric—"

The woman he'd been trapped with had to be one in a billion.

His eyes strayed to the crib. The baby sleeping so peacefully was his son. It was unbelievable! Throwing off his own shock, he walked over to the crib and looked down at the baby—*his baby*—lying on his back with his arms outstretched, his hands formed into fists.

"In spite of all that death and destruction coming for us, we managed to produce a son!"

"Yes." She'd joined him. "Incredibly, he's perfect."

Ric had thought the same thing the second he'd laid eyes on him. In that moment he'd suffered pain thinking his parent had fathered such a beautiful child with *her*. Ric had been so convinced of it that he was still having trouble getting a handle on his emotions.

But it wasn't his father's— It was his own!

His elation was so overpowering, he reached for the baby and held him against his shoulder, uncaring that he'd wake him up again. Ric *wanted* him to wake up so he could get a good look at him. Warmth from the little bundle seeped into his body's core, bonding them as father and son.

The baby must have sensed someone different was holding him. He started wiggling and moved his dark silky head from side to side. He smelled sweet like his mother. He was such a strong little thing that Ric was forced to support his head and neck with more strength. He lowered him in the crook of his arm so he could pick out the unique features that proclaimed him a Degenoli and an Argyle. Both sets of genes were unmistakable.

"*Ciao, bambino mio.* Welcome to my world." He kissed his cheeks and forehead. His olive-skinned baby grew more animated. Ric laughed when those arms and legs moved and kicked with excitement. The *first* Degenoli in this generation to live.

His sister, Claudia, had barely learned she was pregnant before she'd suffered a miscarriage. It had happened soon after she'd heard their father had been killed in the avalanche. His sorrow for her and her husband, Marco's, loss would always hurt, but as he looked down at his son, there wasn't room in his soul for anything but joy.

When Ric looked up, he caught Sami's tear-filled eyes fastened on the two of them. After wondering what she'd looked like, he couldn't get his fill of staring at her.

"I can't fathom it that you're alive, that you're holding him," she cried. "When I left the police station, I was heartbroken. If I didn't find Alberto in Geneva, it meant going home knowing my baby would never know the Italian side of his family. What if you hadn't followed me here?" she cried.

"Nothing could have stopped me. I had to find out who

you really were because I couldn't believe there was another woman alive who sounded like you."

"I know what you mean. The second you spoke to me, I should have stopped trying to be cautious and just called you Ric to see what you'd do. It would have saved us both so much trouble."

Ric would have responded, but his cell phone rang. It jerked him back to reality. He had a strong idea who it was.

"I'll take the baby while you answer it." Sami plucked the baby out of his arms and walked the floor with him.

He watched his little boy burrow his head in her neck. The action brought a lump to his throat before he wheeled away from her and checked the caller ID. Though he'd finally come to the end of his search for the woman named Sami, time had passed during that search and other dynamics had been set in motion.

Ric groaned when he thought of how this news was going to affect negotiations with Eliana's father, let alone with Eliana herself. Theirs was no love match, but news of an unknown baby would be difficult for any bride-to-be to handle. He'd need to deal with her carefully. As for his own family, they would be in shock.

"Eliana?" he said after clicking on.

"I thought you would call me before you left the office, but your secretary said you weren't there."

He rubbed the back of his neck absently. "I'm on my way to the airport and planned to phone you before my jet took off." It would have been the truth if something else hadn't come up. Something that had changed the very fabric of his life. The Sami he'd been entombed with was alive and had just presented him with his *son!*

There was a distinct pause. "Are you all right? You sound…different."

Different didn't begin to cover what was going on inside him.

"It's…business. I'm afraid I'm preoccupied with it. Forgive me." It was the kind of business Chief Coretti had referred to at the station. But it had everything to do with Ric, not with his father. When he thought of the way his suspicious mind had worked trying to get answers…

"Of course I forgive you, Enrico."

Ric took a steadying breath. Before they were married, those words were going to be put to the test in the cruelest of ways.

Sami had called him a great man. How honorable did it make him if he kept this revelation from Eliana? But he couldn't tell her yet. It wasn't possible when he could hardly comprehend it himself. With this news there would be so many ramifications, he needed time to think how he was going to handle everything.

"I'll phone you from Cyprus tomorrow."

"That had better be a promise."

He gripped the phone tighter. "Have I ever broken one to you?"

"No, but I'm still angry you've let business interfere so much. After we're married I intend to keep you occupied for a long time. For one thing, I want to give you a baby. Hopefully a male heir."

Ric closed his eyes tightly. *Someone got ahead of you in that department, Eliana.*

His fiancée was a beautiful, polished product of her aristocratic upbringing. He couldn't fault his future wife for voicing her womanly expectations. But neither could he do anything about the new state of affairs. Fate had blown in with the avalanche, altering his world forever.

"Forgive me, Eliana, but I have to go. We'll talk tomorrow."

"A domani, Caro."

He ended the call and turned to Sami.

The baby had fallen asleep against her shoulder. She eyed Ric steadily. "While you were on the phone, I've had time to gather my thoughts. Maybe I'm wrong, but I sensed a woman was on the other end of that phone call. Judging by the tone of your voice, she's either your wife or your girlfriend."

During those hours they'd been trapped, they'd crossed all the boundaries waiting for the end. It didn't surprise Ric she wasn't only intuitive, but forthright. "My fiancée, Eliana."

Not one dark eyelash flickered. "Were you—"

"No." He knew what was on her mind. "I didn't get engaged to her until long after I'd lost all hope of ever finding you. I kept the thought alive that since I'd told you my last name, you might come back to Genoa to look for me. Now that I understand you were carrying our son all that time, I know why you didn't come until now."

"Did you ever tell your fiancée about us?"

"Not her, not anyone," he whispered before moving closer. "Are you involved with someone? Married?"

"No." Her single-word answer shouldn't have filled him with relief, but it did. "I'd just broken up with a man I'd been dating before I left for Europe on my trip in January. As you can imagine, I wasn't the same person when I returned.

"When Matt found out I was back, he called me and told me he hadn't given up on us." Ric could understand why. "I told him it was over for me, but he said he was going to keep trying to get through to me. When I discovered I was pregnant, I told him the truth of what happened to me in Italy so he'd give up."

Ric bit down hard. "And did he?"

"No. He said he'd marry me and help me raise the baby as if it were his own."

The idea of another man parenting Ric's son didn't sit well with him. "He must love you very much."

"Yes, I believe he does. I love him, too. He's really wonderful, but I'm not in love with him. There's a huge difference. That why I broke up with him in the first place, because I didn't want to hurt him.

"He's been very good to me, but I know it hurt him horribly that I would make love with a stranger, especially when he and I hadn't gotten to that point." Her voice faltered. "No matter how I tried to explain the circumstances, I realized it sounded incredible."

"It still does," Ric confessed. "Even to me, and I was there."

Color crept back into her cheeks. "It would be asking

too much of him to forget it. I know he's still hoping I'll change my mind, but I can't see that happening." She kissed the baby. "How soon is your wedding?"

The wedding to Eliana...

"January first."

"New Year's—that's coming soon."

With Sami standing there cuddling his son, Ric found it impossible to think about his upcoming nuptials. The shock still hadn't worn off.

Her eyes searched his. "I realize it isn't every day a man is confronted with a situation like ours—" she said anxiously. "If I'd known you were alive, I would have handled everything differently. But now that you know you have a son, I'm aware you need time for the information to settle in before you can tell how you really feel about everything."

"How I feel?" he questioned, not understanding the remark. "You've just presented me with my child. I didn't know that being a father would bring me this kind of happiness."

Neither Ric nor his siblings had ever been close to their father. He was gone so much, they rarely saw him. Though he'd ruled over their family, he left the child-rearing to their mother and the house staff.

Not until college did his father take an interest in Ric. Even then it was all about duty and money. When Ric thought about how his father had always ignored Vito and Claudia, his insides twisted into knots. Early on he'd decided that if he were ever to become a father, he'd get totally involved in his children's lives from day one.

For Ric, today *was* day one. He eyed the mother of his child. "I didn't know learning I was a father would make me feel reborn in a whole new way."

"Nevertheless, you're getting married before long and have all this to talk over with Eliana," she said in a pragmatic tone. "It's a good thing my flight for the States leaves in the morning. Ric and I will go back to Reno while you let this sink in. Now that we know of each other's existence and can exchange phone numbers, there's no hurry."

He frowned. "No hurry? I've missed the first two months of my son's life and don't intend to miss any more."

"But with Christmas and your wedding almost here, this isn't the time to—"

"To what?" He cut her off. "Decide how to fit our baby into my life? He wasn't conceived on your schedule or mine, but he's a living breathing miracle. Unlike my father, who hardly acknowledged the existence of his children until they were grown, I want to be with my son all the time that you and I can work out."

Her face closed up. "There's nothing to work out the way you mean. We live on separate continents. He's my reason for living. After you and Eliana are married, I'll bring him for visits the way I would have done if your father had been the one who was alive. My sister will help me so the flights won't be expensive. When it's possible, you and your wife can fly to the States to see him."

Ric was listening, but the woman who'd given birth to his child was still a stranger to him in ways he had yet to understand. However, that was about to change, because he had no intention of letting her fly out of his life with their son.

CHAPTER THREE

"We'll talk about that later. For now we need to get better acquainted." Already he sensed she would require careful handling first. "I'm on my way to my second home on Cyprus to do vital business, so I'm taking you there with me tonight."

Her eyes widened in surprise.

"You said you wanted Ric to know about the Italian side of his family. My mother came from Cyprus. I spent most of my childhood there. As Ric grows older, it will be his second home, too. I want you to be with me for the next week and see my world in relaxed surroundings. It has the warmest climate in the Mediterranean during the winter months. Tomorrow it's supposed to hit seventy degrees, warm enough to go swimming."

She let out a small cry. "I couldn't do that, Ric. I only intended to be here a few days."

His body stiffened. "But you didn't know you'd find *me*. Now that you have, everything's changed for both of us. Our baby needs to be with his family. If your sister can't rearrange your flight for a different day, *I* can."

"I've no doubt of it," she conceded, "*if* you didn't have a fiancée who won't understand."

"She isn't expecting me back until Christmas Eve day. Until then, what I do with my time while I'm not in Genoa is my business. You and I have to talk things through. For you to go home tomorrow is out of the question."

"But—"

"Sami—" he broke in. "You wouldn't refuse me this time with you and the son I didn't know I had. We need time together to process the fact that the three of us are alive." He sucked in his breath. "We were given a second chance, not only to live life but to rejoice together in our beautiful son."

"Still—"

"There's no *still* about it. After what happened to us at that resort in Imst, I'm not taking any chances of another unexpected disaster. Anything could go wrong on your way back to Reno. Don't say it wouldn't happen, because we know better. I need this time with you and Ric. Be honest and admit you need it, too, now that you know I'm alive."

Sami looked away. "Even so, your fiancée will be devastated when she finds out the truth. How long do you plan to keep her in the dark?"

His eyes narrowed on her features. "For as long as it takes. I don't have a better answer."

"I'm afraid for her, Ric. I saw how the news affected Matt and we weren't even dating anymore. The revelation about the baby will be so terrible for her, she might never recover from it, especially if you don't tell her right away. I know if I were in her shoes and—"

"Let's not anticipate what might or might not happen," he interrupted her. "Your boyfriend heard the truth and told you he still wants to marry you."

"Maybe, maybe not," she answered honestly. "I told him I needed time and haven't seen him in months. But if we did get together for the sake of the baby, I'm afraid that over time he would learn to resent me for what I did. He wants children one day.

"If we married, it would be normal for him to love a son or daughter of his own body more than he loved Ric. I couldn't bear for that to happen. That's been one of the things holding me back from getting involved again. I won't let anything hurt Ric if I can help it."

"I hear what you're saying, Sami." He loved it that she guarded their son's happiness so fiercely. "I have those same protective feelings. That's why I have to be careful before I tell Eliana anything. She'll be hurt in ways I can promise not even *you* have thought of yet."

She shook her head. "This is such an incredible situation."

"But not insoluble. Ric's been your first priority or you wouldn't have flown to Genoa to find his grandfather. Now that I know of his existence, he's *my* first priority. I want to get up in the night and feed him. Over the next week I want to bathe him and do all those things a new father does. In that amount of time I'll know better how to approach my fiancée."

"I—I'd feel better if Eliana knew I was with you," she stammered. "What if someone tells her?"

"Who? My staff and pilot are all loyal to me. Chief Coretti knows better than to discuss my business with anyone."

"Even so, I—"

"Even so nothing— Unlike you, I haven't had the advantage of nine months to think things through while waiting for the arrival of our baby. Once I've spent time with you and Ric, I'll be better equipped to know how to deal with Eliana and anticipate her questions. For you to turn around and fly back to Reno in the morning would be a knee-jerk reaction that will only complicate our situation."

She still wouldn't look at him. He admired her for wanting to protect Eliana, but the baby was a fact of life. While they'd clung together in the claustrophobic darkness, he'd made her pregnant. Little Ric was their creation. Despite the fallout when the news surfaced, the knowledge filled him with a wonder and excitement he'd never known before.

He darted her a glance. "The remarkable woman I was buried with wouldn't begrudge me those privileges. Has she changed so much in eleven months?"

That brought her head up. "But you're not prepared for a baby."

"Is anyone? If you're talking about his physical needs, you've brought everything he requires with you for the moment. Whatever is missing, I'll take care of it. With one phone call, a crib and bedding can be delivered."

"I don't know, Ric." She still wasn't convinced.

"Don't tell me you're uncomfortable with me, not after everything we've been through?"

A faint flush filled her cheeks. "No. Of course not."

"Then there's nothing to stop you from agreeing to come with me. I'll have one of my men check you out of the hotel."

She eyed him in confusion. "Who are they exactly?"

"My bodyguards."

"I remember you telling me you were in shipping. What I don't understand is why you would need that kind of protection."

"I'll explain later."

"But you're not ready for guests," she argued, "especially not an infant."

"Guests?" he exploded. "Ric's my son, and you're his mother. That puts you in an entirely different category from anyone else in the world. Would you rather I stayed here with you for the next week?"

"You mean at the hotel?"

He heard panic in her voice and realized with satisfaction that she wasn't any more indifferent to him than he was to her. "I mean in this room. After all you've gone through to find my father, do you honestly think I'd budge from here without you?"

"I thought you had vital business on Cyprus," she said quietly.

"My son is the only business more vital. I thought I'd made myself clear. But keep in mind that on the island you'll have your own bedroom with the Mediterranean only steps outside your suite. We'll set up a crib next to you where you and Ric can live in total comfort. But we can stay right here if that's your wish. The decision is up to you."

She pressed her lips together, further evidence she didn't like either option. "When were you going to leave?"

"Two hours ago. A limo is parked for me in front of the hotel."

He waited while she mulled everything over in her mind. "I'm frightened," she finally whispered.

"The woman who sought help from Genoa's chief of police to find Ric's grandfather was a warrior. It pleases me more than you know to realize my son has inherited that trait from you."

"You don't know that," she answered shakily.

Ric shifted his weight. "What do you think are the chances of a fetus to survive what you lived through both emotionally and physically?"

Her haunted gaze collided with his, giving him his answer. "If you'll get your things together, I'll take them down. It's a few hours' flight to Paphos. Once we're in the air, we'll have dinner. I don't know about you, but I'm famished."

She looked at the baby, then glanced back at him. "If you're sure about this," she murmured.

"I've never been more sure of anything in my life."

After another long hesitation, she walked over to a closet for her suitcase. With that action, the tautness left his body. He pulled out his cell phone to call his house-keeper in Paphos and give her some instructions. While he waited for Sami to finish her small amount of packing, he spoke to Carlo and the driver, alerting them to his plans.

Earlier, on the drive to the hotel from the police station, he'd entertained the thought that his father had indulged in an affair with this woman. No way on earth could he have known that Christine Argyle would turn out to be *Sami*. Even more astounding was the knowledge that the baby he'd heard crying from behind the door was none other than his own son.

Sami's legs felt shaky. The mixture of shock and hunger had reduced her to this state. For Ric to be alive didn't seem possible, yet here he was, this tall, hard-muscled Italian male who held the baby to his shoulder with one arm, and carried her suitcase in his other hand.

But he had a fiancée! The news of it flickered off and on like a giant neon sign. How could she just go along with him like this knowing he belonged to someone else? She'd tried to reason with him, but he'd refused to listen to her fears.

"This is heavy," he said in an aside, oblivious to her state of mind. "What's in here?"

"Baby formula. I had to bring a lot in case of an emergency."

He broke out in laughter, causing people to stare. She walked alongside him holding the car seat and diaper bag. For all the world the three of them looked like a married couple staying at the hotel for the Christmas holiday, yet the woman he intended to marry was somewhere in Genoa, not knowing what had happened.

Sami's guilt was so overwhelming, she barely noticed that the hotel had been festively decorated for Christmas. All she sensed was Ric's pride as hotel guests and staff alike smiled to see him carrying his baby.

She also saw the envy in the eyes of women young and old who found Ric drop-dead gorgeous. That's what he was. A thrill darted through her to realize their son would grow up to look like him. It was followed by another stab of guilt to be thinking about him like this when he had a fiancée.

When he ushered her through the main doors to the outside, he'd said his car was waiting. But there were no cars parked in front, only three black luxury limousines. The center one had special smoked glass and a hood ornament with a unique gold figure of what looked like an ancient seaman.

Two of Ric's bodyguards opened the doors to help her inside and deal with the luggage, including securing the car seat into place, with little Ric firmly settled into it. Their deference to him caused her to stare into his inky-black eyes once they were seated across from each other. The limo started moving. "Ric? What's going on?"

"We're heading to the airport." His deep voice oozed through her body, kindling her senses without her volition.

"But in *this?*"

"You're not comfortable?" Behind his hooded gaze she thought he might be smiling in amusement.

"That question doesn't deserve an answer. Why did the driver address you as Excellency? I may not understand Italian, but I heard him distinctly, so don't tell me I misunderstood. Are you an important government official?"

He kissed the top of the baby's head. Ric was still sound asleep. "My business is shipping, remember?"

She expelled the breath she'd been holding. "You do a great deal more than that! Who are you? Please tell me the truth." He could be a terrible tease, something she hadn't expected. Though they'd shared the most intimate experience between two people, she knew next to nothing about him…except the most important thing.

He was a man of character who'd welcomed his son without hesitation, even though he was engaged to be married. How many men would do that?

"I'm Alberto Enrico Degenoli the thirteenth."

"All of your predecessors had the same name?"

"Yes."

She made a sound that came out more like a squeal. "That's very interesting, but I know you haven't told me everything. When we were buried, you never said a word about any of this."

One black brow lifted. "You never mentioned you were a student or where you were enrolled. If you'd told me, I could have found you months ago."

If by those words he meant that their lives might be different, it was too late now! Her body trembled. "If you recall, we decided we shouldn't talk much."

"True. Instead we communicated in a more fundamental way under the most death-defying circumstances.

I believe making love in total blackness added a thrilling element that increased our pleasure, thus producing our son."

With those words, the memory of what had transpired caused her body to break out in feverish heat.

"One day," Ric continued, "he'll be indebted to us for giving him life against those odds, don't you agree? I know I'll be undyingly grateful to you for taking such meticulous care of him in my absence, Sami."

Though she was warmed by his compliment, the implication that his absence was now over rocked her to the core. She'd heard the steel behind it. Chief Coretti had jumped the moment Ric had suggested he leave the room. His own office! Come to think of it, the police chief had been able to locate Ric immediately. On the verge of asking him one more time who he really was, Sami was distracted by the limo coming to a stop.

"We've arrived," he murmured. On cue the doors opened for them.

She climbed out to see a gleaming green-and-white private jet with the word "Degenoli" printed in gold on the side with a logo of a mariner beneath it. Before she knew it, one of his staff escorted her to the jet with her luggage. She started up the steps with Ric right behind her holding the baby.

The steward showed her to one of the posh white leather seats in the club compartment. Ric strapped the car seat into the seat between them, then settled the baby, who'd fallen asleep again. As soon as she sat down, the

Fasten Seatbelts sign flashed on. Soon the engines started up and the jet began to taxi out to the runway.

Though she knew she wasn't living in a dream, the revelations of this day were still unreal to her. When she really thought about her and Ric being alone together again for a whole week, her body shivered with a barrage of new sensations.

She should have phoned Pat in Reno to tell her everything, but Ric was like a force of nature. Everything had happened too fast. Now wasn't the time to get into a conversation with her sister while Ric sat nearby, able to listen. But when they landed in Paphos and got settled, she'd make the call.

Pat was in for the biggest surprise of her life. She would have fits when she heard Ric had a fiancée who still didn't know about the baby.

When the jet reached cruising speed and the seatbelt light went off, the steward served them a delicious pasta and chicken dinner accompanied by a sweet white wine. After Sami took a sip, Ric eyed her intently. "I take it you aren't nursing."

Sami put the glass down. "I tried it, but my milk jaundiced him, so the pediatrician told me to put him on formula. He loves it at room temperature and has been a good eater from the beginning."

His gaze wandered back to the baby. "I noticed he drank every drop of his bottle back at the hotel. I'm eager to feed him when he wakes up again."

Little Ric must have heard his father's voice because it wasn't a minute before he opened his eyes and started making sounds. That was all Ric needed to release the baby from the seat and nestle him in his arms.

Having finished her dinner, Sami got up and searched in the diaper bag for a new bottle of formula and a clean burping cloth. "It sounds like you're hungry again, sweetheart." She leaned over to kiss his cheeks before handing Ric the bottle. "Just put it in his mouth and he'll do the rest." On that note she placed the toweling cloth over his right shoulder, then sat down again.

Ric laughed as he played with the baby before feeding him. When the steward came in, Ric lifted his son for the other man to look at. They both smiled and spoke in Italian before he took away their dishes.

Sami could see Ric was a natural at being a father. She was the slightest bit jealous their baby seemed content for his daddy to do the honors, but it also touched her heart. Little Ric was wrapped up in his silky blue baby quilt with the white lace around the edge. He made a beautiful picture against his father's tan jacket.

No doubt he wore a custom-made suit produced for him by a famous Italian designer. When they'd clung to each other in the darkness, he'd been wearing a shirt. But whoever said that clothes made the man hadn't met Ric.

Whether in the light or the dark, *he* made the man.

Stop thinking about him like this, Sami. He was about to be someone else's husband.

She felt his eyes flick to hers. "Our son is perfect."

Sami had been thinking the same thing about Ric. Out of all the men in the entire world, how had she happened to be caught in the same avalanche with *him?* "He reminds me of a baby prince in one of my old books of fairy tales."

"Not a prince," Ric corrected her before kissing his son on the cheek. "A count."

She blinked.

"The first Alberto Enrico Degenoli went to sea and amassed a fortune he brought back to Genoa. For that, the ruling power made him a count. Through various ventures in shipping, that fortune grew over the years. Our family history dates back to the thirteenth century."

Sami hadn't thought she could be shocked a second time in one day. Now, when she thought about it, the gold seaman ornament on the hood of the limousine made sense, but too many revelations in just a few hours had her reeling.

Her hands gripped the sides of the chair. Ric was literally Count Degenoli. In a few more weeks his fiancée would be *Countess* Degenoli. Good heavens!

"When you had the baby, you didn't realize you'd given birth to Alberto Enrico Degenoli the Fourteenth. He's my firstborn son. By rights he should be the next count after me."

Sami understood what he meant. That honor would go to the son he and Eliana would produce. Little Ric could never be the next count because he was the *illegitimate* son.

"After my father died, the title passed to me," Ric continued in a conversational tone, "but the title means nothing in this day and age, so forget it, Sami. To his friends, our son will be Ric Argyle Degenoli."

The ramifications of what all this meant made it hard for her to swallow. "Ric—I'm not naive. Knowing you're a count means your engagement is of public importance. Any move on your part will produce a ripple effect with serious consequences."

"You're right, but you agreed to come with me, so no one else knows yet. Later on we'll talk everything over. For the present I intend to enjoy this time with you and our son. Can you let your reservations go that long?"

Some nuance in his tone got to her. Sami bowed her head, attempting to come to grips with this latest revelation. She didn't know if she could do what he asked. But when she tried to put herself in his shoes, she could understand why he needed emotional time away from responsibilities and duties to deal with being a brand-new father.

"There's no precedent for what has happened to us," she admitted at last. "I'm sorry to keep fighting you on it. You're right for reminding me I had the whole pregnancy to realize I was going to be a mother. You only found out this afternoon that you're a father. I'll try to control my anxiety for a few days."

In the silence that followed, he leaned forward and put his hand over hers. She felt heat travel up her arm and through her body. "That sounded like the woman who helped me get through those first horrifying moments when we figured our time was up."

Tears filled her eyes. "I'm so glad it wasn't— Ric's the sweetest, most wonderful thing that ever happened to me."

"We did good work, didn't we?" he said in a husky voice before lifting his hand from hers.

She half laughed. "Yes. My family and friends go crazy over him." Pat had said more than once that the baby's father had to be some kind of Italian god to have produced a child as handsome as Ricky. As Sami eyed Ric covertly, she thought she could tell her sister that Ric was more sensational than any statue. She had to remember that soon he'd be another woman's husband.

"Tell me something. Are you rich?" she teased with a smile.

He kissed the top of Ric's head. "That depends on one's definition."

With a gloomy answer like that, he'd sidestepped the issue. Their son had a father like none other. "Is Eliana's family rich?"

A shadow crossed over his attractive face. "Yes."

Suddenly Ric did a loud burp and they both laughed hard. She was glad to see his father's frown had disappeared. There was nothing like a baby to reduce everything else to the unimportant.

"Forgive me for being curious. I've never known a count before."

"I don't like to be reminded of it, Sami. It's meaningless."

She rolled her eyes. "Not to the men who called you Excellency."

He grimaced. "Old habits die hard."

"I'm glad you told me how you feel. I'll never make

the mistake of calling you count. It will be up to you to tell Ric one day."

Sami heard his sharp intake of breath. "Since you're his mother, I'm going to let you in on a secret no one knows about yet. After my father died, I took the steps to have the title officially abolished. I made it legally binding so that it can never be bestowed on anyone else again, which means Ric's life is going to be free and his children after him."

She studied him anxiously. "Has it been such a burden?"

He flashed her a bleak glance. "You'll never know."

"Tell me about it." *Help me get my mind off the woman you love.*

"The title is always bestowed on the first male heir. It was all I heard about from the moment I can first remember. All the attention was focused on me—my education, my social life, my duties, my future wife. But my siblings were ignored.

"Vito and Claudia were fixtures in the background of our lives. My brother became a shell of himself with no confidence or sense of accomplishment. Claudia was a girl and virtually forgotten in the scheme of things.

"Every time I received an honor from my father, I flinched inside, knowing my brother and sister were left behind and in some cases forgotten."

"How awful," Sami whispered.

"You have no idea. It sickened me and I swore that the day I became count, I'd have the whole reign of terror obliterated. That day came after we buried our father."

Sami thought long and hard about what he'd just told her. Titles were still de rigueur in certain societies, but apparently Ric abhorred the whole idea of them so much, he'd taken steps to rid himself of his title. That took an unusual man with the strength of his own convictions. She admired him more than he would ever know.

His siblings wouldn't have believed at first that he could do such an extraordinary thing, but since he was still the count, he had the right to do as he pleased.

Sami had to admit the title had a certain ring. She secretly treasured the knowledge that when they'd made love, another Count Degenoli had been conceived. A very little one. For the short time left, she could fantasize about how romantic it all sounded.

But that was shameful of her when she knew how diabolical the system clearly was in Ric's eyes. Since the drive to the airport, Sami had felt as though she was living in a fairy tale; she was the young maid—being spirited away by the handsome prince to live in his castle. But there were two important caveats to this tale.

By Christmas Eve the spell would be broken and Sami and her baby would return to Nevada to get on with the rest of their lives. By New Year's Day, Ric would be married.

She sat up straighter in the chair. "What do you think Eliana will say when she finds out your title is gone?"

His answer wasn't a long time in coming. "She'll have to handle it. That's what she's been raised to do."

"Not if it wasn't her dream." For no good reason, her

heart rate accelerated. "When are you planning to let her know?"

"As soon as I receive word. I expected to hear a week ago, but the courts are slower here than in the States."

"I didn't know that was possible."

Another chuckle escaped his throat. "It's my Christmas present to myself, but your gift trumps anything I could have conceived of in this world or the next."

"You can think of Ric as your Christmas baby."

"*Our* baby," he corrected in a thick-toned voice before switching him to his other shoulder. She could see he was totally enamored by his son. Sami could relate. "I believe our little *bimbo* is sleepy."

"Bimbo?"

"It's another Italian endearment."

"That's sweet," she murmured. "He's easy right now because all he basically does is eat and sleep. In another month everything will change."

Ric nuzzled the baby's neck. "Did you hear that, *figlio mio?* How about we change your diaper before you sign out again?"

Sami chuckled as she laid everything out for him. "I know the diaper looks tiny, but it does the job." They smiled at each other before he got down to business. After a little too much powder, and a couple of tries to attach the tapes right, he'd managed to change their son's diaper. "Bravo," she exclaimed.

He picked up the baby and eyed her over his head. "I'll do better next time."

"I can't tell you the number of times I put the diaper on the wrong way. Ric was so patient."

By tacit agreement they both sat down with Ric hugging the baby to his chest. "Tell me about the delivery. Were you in labor long?"

"About eighteen hours."

His eyes grew serious. "Were you alone?"

"No. My sister and her husband took turns staying with me. I owe them everything."

His jaw hardened. "I should have been there. Did you know you were going to have a son ahead of time?"

Her lips curved. "Oh, yes. I called him Ric the second the technician handed me the ultrasound pictures. She told me I had a boy in there and everything looked great. I'll admit I wished you'd been in the room to hear the news with me. While I lay there, I had this fanciful notion that maybe you were watching from above or somehow knew, and I hoped it would make you happy."

"I think you know exactly how I felt when you handed me his birth certificate. It was the supreme moment of my life." The throb in his voice gave evidence how deeply his emotions were involved.

"Ric? Tell me the truth. Was the reason you looked for me because you wanted to know if you'd made me pregnant?"

His gaze wandered over her. "No. To be honest, I was afraid you might have died in the hospital you were taken to. You could have lost consciousness the way I did and never come to. I had to be sure."

"Why?"

"Because if you were alive, I wanted to meet you face-to-face. I wanted to understand why two strangers could connect the way we did. I thought if we talked, maybe I'd get answers to questions that have plagued me ever since."

She made an assenting sound. "I have the same questions, but am no nearer to an explanation. For us, it wasn't a physical attraction in the literal sense of the word. Maybe you'll think I'm crazy, but the only way I can describe it is that our spirits spoke to each other."

"Or recognized each other on some other level?" he inserted.

"Yes, as if we were bidding each other a final farewell which we did with…our bodies."

"I've had the same thoughts, Sami. They're not crazy."

"I'm glad you feel that way because I've gone over and over it in my mind and it's the only conclusion that makes sense." She stirred restlessly. "When I first got back to Oakland, I felt so empty inside. I knew you'd died and I felt this great loss. It alarmed me. It wasn't just the fact that we'd made love. What we did wasn't for the normal reasons. I mean—"

"I know what you mean." He read her mind with ease.

"While we were trapped, I'd assumed we would die. The thought of getting pregnant never entered my consciousness."

"Nor mine," he murmured. "The thought of using protection was the furthest thing from my mind."

"All we knew was that we were facing the end."

"But during those hours, I felt I'd lived a lifetime."

He'd taken the words right out of her mouth. "When I was released from the hospital, at first I thought what I was feeling had to be sadness over the way my father had died. But after a time, I still had that same heaviness. No matter how deeply I searched for the source of it, *you* were always at the bottom of it."

"That's how it was for me, too," she volunteered. "Matt thought I was having some symptoms of post-traumatic stress disorder because of the avalanche. He knew I'd been trapped with you, but I didn't tell him everything at first. I was hoping I'd pull out of whatever was going on inside me. Then I found out I was pregnant."

She glanced at their baby sleeping so trustingly on Ric's chest. "Maybe I shouldn't have been overjoyed by the news, but I was. Of course I had to tell Matt everything. But he never truly understood." After a pause she said, "I can promise you now—Eliana won't understand either."

"No. And once she learns the truth and meets you, she'll assume you're the reason why the physical side of our relationship has been unsatisfactory."

Sami squirmed in her seat. "I shouldn't have come to Genoa."

"You know you don't mean that."

No. She didn't… "For you to be engaged, I'm sure your love can weather anything."

"Sami—I'm not in love with Eliana."

What?

"We're marrying to secure the financial welfare of our two families. Don't get me wrong, Eliana has many admirable qualities and I care for her, but I don't love her. Unfortunately, when I asked her to marry me, I didn't know the 'for worse' part of the ceremony would precede taking our vows."

Sami stirred restlessly. Maybe he didn't love Eliana, but she couldn't imagine Eliana not being head over heels in love with him. What woman wouldn't love him? The knowledge of a baby would tear his fiancée to pieces. Sami was about to question him further when the Fasten Seatbelts sign flashed on. "We're in Cyprus already?"

Ric was on his feet in an instant to secure the baby for the descent. "I told you it's not a long flight. When we step off the plane, you'll notice a difference in the temperature. Whenever I breathe that air, it reminds me of my youth and carefree days. Do you know I haven't taken a real vacation here in a long time?"

"Not even with your fiancée?"

"She's never been here. Eliana's not fond of the water. But now that you're with me, I'm ready for one."

"But you've come on business."

"I'm capable of doing both."

CHAPTER FOUR

SAMI had barely paused for breath since meeting Ric again. Who would have thought a few short hours could have changed so much in her life? Now she and little Ric had flown on Count Degenoli's private jet to an exotic island in the Mediterranean. Whether right or wrong, she was too physically and emotionally exhausted to think about the wisdom of her decision to come with him. Tomorrow would be soon enough to face the consequences of her actions.

The drive from Paphos airport hadn't taken long before the car entered a flower-lined private estate isolated on a point overlooking the water. Within ten minutes Ric was showing Sami through a fabulous, white, two-story Grecian villa. The colorful Mediterranean furnishings against white walls caught her eye everywhere she looked.

A cushion of blue here, an urn of yellow with an exotic plant there, an unexpected Greek icon in predominantly red and gold colors around the corner. So many choice armoires and tables placed around on tiled floors with a definite flair revealed a luxurious treasure trove.

Beyond the villa was the sight of the water through the window and doorways. Ric's second home was paradise. Sami could only imagine the elegance of his first home.

She marveled that his staff had managed to buy a crib so fast and have it set up in one of the guest rooms on the second floor. Besides fresh flowers, they'd provided everything needed to make her and the baby comfortable. To her delight each room of the villa contained a charming Christmas crèche surrounded by lighted candles. Ric explained that Christmas trees weren't amongst their local traditions.

He introduced her to Mara and Daimon, an older couple, probably in their sixties. He told her they'd been living here taking care of the villa and grounds for years. They'd worked for Ric's mother's family and spoke good English.

When Ric showed them the baby, the dark-haired couple cried out in delight and took turns holding him. Whatever they thought about Ric bringing home a foreign woman and a child, they didn't let it show and honored him like the favorite son he evidently was.

Mara smiled at Sami. "Anything you want, you ask me."

"I will. Thank you."

"The little one is beautiful, like you. He has your mouth."

"You're very kind. I think he looks like his father."

Daimon nodded. "I knew he was a Degenoli the minute I saw him."

"I see Vito in him," Ric inserted.

"A little," Mara said. "He also has Claudia's shell-like ears, but his shape and size and those brilliant black eyes are all yours, Enrico."

Daimon nodded. "He's well named."

Sami glanced at him. "What does it mean?"

"Ruler of the household."

Ric's black orbs kindled with warmth as he studied their son. "For now he's our *piccolo*."

"There's another word I don't understand."

"It means little one."

"That's a darling endearment for him," she exclaimed, "especially the way you say it in such beautiful soft Italian. Your language has lots of words I love to say, like *ciao* and *cappuccino*." She'd emphasized the *chee* sound, causing him to chuckle.

Sami noticed an aura had come over him since they'd entered the house, as if he'd dropped his worries outside the door. She couldn't deny he looked happier. In truth he no longer resembled the intimidating male at the police station in the tan silk suit who'd glared at her with barely suppressed hostility the moment she'd walked in.

All of a sudden his gaze swerved to hers with concern. "It's almost midnight. You must be dead on your feet. If there's anything you'd like to eat or drink, Mara will bring it to you before we say goodnight."

She shook her head. "After that meal on the plane, I couldn't, but thank you anyway."

"What you and the baby need is a good sleep after your flight from Genoa." Mara kissed little Ric on the cheek before she and Daimon disappeared to their room at the back of the villa on the main floor.

Sami turned to Ric. "They're wonderful."

"They're like family to me. I trust them with my life. Our baby will be pampered and spoiled while we're here."

"What a lucky little boy. I'll just bathe him and put him down, then get ready for bed."

"I'd like to do the honors if you'll show me how." He led them upstairs to her guest room.

"You're not too exhausted?"

He gave her a speculative look. "I'm so wired, as you Americans say, I don't know when I'll be able to sleep."

She let out a gentle laugh. "Then bring the diaper bag into the bathroom and we'll get started. He loves the water."

"That's because he's a true Degenoli. The first one went to sea and now seawater runs through all our veins." His comment made her chuckle. As for the pride in his voice, it was something to witness.

"We'll have to be careful not to keep him in too long or his fingers will start to look like dried grapes." Ric's burst of laughter rang throughout the villa. "Go ahead and undress him while I fill the sink."

They worked in harmony. When the temperature felt right she said, "Lower him in the water and let him enjoy it."

It tugged at her heart to see the care he took with the baby, who got terribly excited. He wiggled and moved his arms and legs with sheer enjoyment as the water lapped around him. In the middle of so much pleasure, the baby urinated, creating a fountain that had Ric's shoulders shaking with silent laughter.

She couldn't hold back her own giggles. "As you can see, his plumbing works just fine. We'll have to start this again." While Ric held the baby in a towel, she let out the water and put some more in. His little chin quivered from leaving the warmth. He was so adorable. Soon he was lowered back in.

"This is glycerin soap to wash his hair and body. It's gentle. He needs his hair washed. Be sure and get into the creases around his neck and behind his ears where the milk runs."

While he did a pretty masterful job for a beginner, she set out a fresh towel ready to dry the baby.

"He's strong, Sami."

"Of course. He's what we Americans call a 'chip off the old block.' Not that you're an old block, but you know what I mean."

His eyes glinted as they shared a silent look of mutual understanding. This time he powdered his son just the right amount and diapered him without any problem. Sami got out a yellow stretchy suit. Ric fitted him into it and fastened the snaps.

"He's almost finished." She handed Ric the little hairbrush. He took it from her and played with the baby's soft hair for a minute.

When he was through, he lifted Ric and turned him to her. "What do you think, *mamma?*"

The use of the Italian version of *mommy* caught her by the throat. Everything felt so natural, she'd forgotten she was a guest in his house. She'd almost forgotten he had a fiancée who had no idea what was going on.

"No one would know you'd only learned you were a father today. He loved his bath with you. I have a feeling he's going to want you to do it all the time. Our baby likes the masculine touch, don't you, sweetheart?"

Sami had already gotten past her jealousy into an area where she was enjoying this way too much. Judging from the emotion streaming from Ric's eyes, he had the same problem. However it was one thing to bathe the baby with Sami looking on, and quite another to imagine Eliana helping him after they were married. Pain filled her chest at the thought of it.

Little Ric was so loveable, but it would take a super-human woman to love him when she hadn't given birth to him. Eliana's resentment toward Sami would always be there because she wasn't the mother of Ric's firstborn child, count or no count. It would boil beneath the surface and the baby would pick up on the tension.

Over the years Sami had met women who were making successes of their second marriages. But it was a struggle combining two families to form a new one. Sami's situation couldn't be compared to theirs. For one thing, she and Ric had been strangers, not husband and wife.

For another, Eliana hadn't had children yet. Her whole life had been lived in preparation for marriage to an aristocrat, a marriage in which the bearing of children was bound to be of the greatest importance, especially the first one. Ric might not want to be Count Degenoli, but

Sami knew in her heart it was part of who he was. Eliana was in for a double shock when she heard the title had been abolished. Sami felt horribly sorry for her.

Deep in thought, she handed Ric a fresh bottle of formula. "While you feed him, I'll clean up the bathroom and take a shower before bed."

Ric stood where he was, snuggling the baby, who was looking for his bottle. "Where did you go just now?" His voice may have been quiet, but she heard the demand in it.

Maybe it was a case of both of them having an extra dose of ESP in their makeup. He was keyed in to her thoughts far too easily.

"I'm pretty sure you know," she answered in a dull tone. "But as you said earlier, let's not get into it right now. This is a time to enjoy the baby. Do what you want with him. Since your room is across the hall from this one, you'll probably hear him cry in the night. If you want to feed him, feel free to come in my bedroom and get a new bottle out of the diaper bag. I'll leave the door open."

His veiled eyes played over her features until her legs shook. "Sleep well, Sami," he murmured before leaving the bathroom with the baby. She shut the door after him and leaned against it, waiting for the weakness to pass. To her alarm, it never did.

Ric had only seen Sami in her suit and blouse. When she walked into the breakfast room at ten the next morning dressed in jeans and a chocolate-colored top, he caught himself staring. Slowly his gaze dropped from her green-eyed blond beauty to the gorgeous mold of her body. His intimate knowledge of her eleven months ago would always be fresh in his mind, and made the visual reaction to her now a hundred times stronger, forcing him to look away.

"Well, look at you two!" She made a nosedive for the baby, who was lying in the carrycot Ric had set on the breakfast table so he could play with him.

"I just fed him his morning bottle, but he hasn't fallen asleep yet. It's giving us time to get better acquainted."

She came around to kiss the baby's face. "Are you having fun with your daddy? Is he already reading the newspaper to you while he enjoys his coffee? If he could talk, he'd probably be calling you *Daddy*. How do you say it in Italian?"

"Papa."

"That's what Pat and I called our grandfather!"

Her enthusiasm caused the baby to grow more animated and made Ric smile. While he watched her poke his son's tummy gently, he inhaled her peach fragrance. She'd just come from the shower. It took all the willpower he possessed not to grab hold of her womanly hips and pull her down on his lap.

"He loves mornings and usually stays awake for a while," she chatted. "No doubt being with you has stimulated him so much, he might not close his eyes till much later." She glanced at Ric. "Has he been good?"

"I think you already know the answer to that question."

She looked away first and sat down on one of the

chairs opposite him. He got the impression she was nervous about getting too close to him. How ironic after what they'd experienced in Austria. "I didn't hear him cry in the night."

"You were exhausted. When I saw you lying there, I realized you'd had the whole care of our son these last two months and no one to wait on you or give you relief."

"I could never complain. Having a baby has been the joy of my life."

"Not all women feel that way," he muttered. Sami was so hands-on with little Ric, he couldn't help but wonder what kind of a mother Eliana would be.

"Do you and your fiancée plan to have children?"

"Definitely. It's what I've been looking forward to most."

"Some men don't want to be fathers."

Ric knew a few like that, but his own father fitted into a different category. He'd wanted an heir, but didn't want to do the fathering that should have gone on. As Ric played with his baby's toes, he realized his father had been the loser on every count.

His mind wandered to Sami. What if this ex-boyfriend Matt stayed so persistent, she ended up marrying him? What kind of a stepfather would he be to little Ric? More and more he didn't like the idea of it.

"Did you get up with him?" she asked.

Her question jerked him out of his dark thoughts. "I did. Around four I thought I heard him fussing. He needed a complete diaper change."

Sami grinned. "Uh-oh. How did your first solo experience go?"

"We made it through, didn't we, *piccolo?*" The baby's tiny fingers still clung to his little finger. They were the same shape as his. He realized no force on earth was as strong as the pull of that miniature hand on his heart. Ric found he didn't want his son to hold on to any other man's finger but his. Until now he hadn't understood how possessive he'd already become over what was his by fatherly right.

Mara walked into the room to refresh Ric's coffee. "Good morning, Sami. Now that you're up, I'll serve breakfast. Coffee for you, too?"

"Just juice if you have some. Please don't go to any trouble."

"How could you be trouble?" she cried. "You won't let me do anything for you, and the *bambino* never cries. I've been waiting for the excuse to hold him!"

"Don't worry," Sami said. "Before long you'll hear him loud and clear. You have my permission to grab him. Just remember his cries can be quite terrifying."

The housekeeper laughed before going out of the room.

"She likes you, Sami."

"That's because she loves you, and therefore loves your son, who I must admit is irresistible."

So is Sami. The unexpected things she said and did had the alarming ability to charm him. Maybe that's why he'd found himself making love to her in the blackness of the avalanche.

At the time he hadn't thought of what she might look like. She was young and afraid, and all he knew was gratitude that he didn't have to die alone. They'd needed each other and taken comfort from each other before they'd both lost consciousness.

It wasn't until he awoke in the hospital and remembered everything that he wanted to find her, talk to her. He was naturally curious to see what the woman looked like who'd helped save his sanity. But it never occurred to him she would be so physically appealing.

When she'd walked into Chief Coretti's office yesterday, he'd found himself attracted to the blond stranger beyond a normal interest in a good-looking woman. Ric had known and been with a number of beautiful women in his life, his fiancée being one of them. But this attraction was different.

The fact that she'd instigated the meeting with the police chief while being so secretive about his father should have been a total turnoff for Ric, but the opposite had held true. She had that spark not given to many people.

As they sat there at the breakfast table, Ric realized the chemistry he felt for her was growing stronger, something that wasn't supposed to happen. Bringing her to Cyprus might have been a mistake after all.

He still needed to phone Eliana, but had been putting it off. Once he heard his fiancée's voice, the magic of this time with Sami and his infant son would evaporate. He wasn't ready for that yet.

Already the baby was his whole life. It had happened the instant he'd walked over to the crib in the hotel room and had seen him lying there so small and helpless. The Degenoli likeness had only increased his wonder.

While he was immersed in thought, Mara had served them. By the time they'd eaten, he'd come up with a plan to stay busy. It would prevent him from thinking too much. Ric refused to think right now and wanted simply to relish this fleeting time.

"Sami? How would you like to take a boat ride in the cabin cruiser?"

"That sounds wonderful!"

"Good. You'll be able to see Paphos from the water. The sea is calm and the air is getting warmer by the minute. Ric will love it. We have swimming costumes and wetsuits on board for your enjoyment. We'll take Daimon and Mara with us."

She lowered her glass. "Did you hear that, sweetheart? We're going on an adventure. We'll have to dress you in your little green sweater and overalls."

Just like that, she'd gone along with Ric without voicing a reservation. Her eagerness to fall in with his plan could mean several things. If she'd wanted a distraction to push her fears away, then he'd just provided an outlet. But if she was nervous being around him for any length of time because she found herself attracted to him, too, he was curious to find out, even though it was the last thing he should be thinking about.

He phoned Daimon and asked him and Mara to join them, then he carried Ric upstairs into her bedroom to get him dressed. Afterward he went to his room and slipped on his bathing trunks and a T-shirt.

Between them, they gathered everything they'd need and headed out of the house for the boat dock. While she held Ric, he found life preservers for all of them. After putting them on, they climbed in. Daimon helped push off before joining Mara at the back of the boat.

Ric's cruiser had a galley and a roof. Both provided shelter for the baby. To his satisfaction Sami sat next to him on the padded bench while he took the wheel. Once he undid the ropes, he idled out to the buoy, then opened up the throttle and they whizzed through the peaceful blue water. Ric kept looking at his son who was wide-awake.

"Do you think he likes it?" he asked her.

Sami smiled at him. "You're asking me when he already has seawater running through his veins?" Ric's white smile turned her heart over. "I'm sure the sound and the vibration have him enthralled."

"How about you?"

"I adore the water, but it's been a long time. This is pure luxury. I've been to Europe several times with Pat and her husband, but never this far south. Cyprus is beautiful."

"It's full of history." He pointed to the city in the distance. "This is the new Paphos. My mother's family home is there."

"Who lives there now?"

"My uncle and his family. It may interest you to know there's an old city there, too. It dates back three thousand years to the Mycenaean period. One of the big attractions is the Temple of Aphrodite."

"The Greek myths! We had to study them in my high-school English class. I loved them. But *you* grew up with them. What a playground you've had here and in Genoa. As I told you before, my grandparents raised Pat and me. Growing up in Oakland we had a view of San Francisco Bay, but here the sea is at your doorstep."

"I confess I love being able to walk out of my house to the water."

"Who wouldn't?" Her voice trailed.

"Tell me what happened to your parents?"

"They were on the freeway driving home when an earthquake hit. We were little girls and don't remember them, but our grandparents kept them alive for us."

"I'm sorry for your loss. Tell me about them." He cut the engine before turning to her.

"Dad was a chemical engineer and Mom stayed home to raise us. I grew up thinking I'd like to follow in his footsteps, but discovered I like computers, too. A year ago last fall I started graduate school to become a computer engineer. If there's been any one thing lacking in my life, it's been the loss of parents I never knew.

"Growing up I envied my friends who had moms and dads. Don't get me wrong. I adored my grandparents, but in a just world, nothing takes the place of a loving, caring parent."

"*Loving* and *caring* being the operative words," Ric mused aloud. More than ever he was determined to be there for his son no matter the obstacles.

He rubbed the side of his jaw. "When you first mentioned your studies, I assumed you were talking about your undergraduate studies. I'm impressed you're pursuing your career while being an exceptional mother at the same time. You have fire in you, Sami, a very rare thing."

She broke into an unguarded smile. "Flattery will get you everywhere."

"It's the truth," he came back. "What brought you to Europe that last time?"

"During the winter break in January, Pat gave me a free pass for a short trip to Innsbruck. I knew if I didn't go, I wouldn't get another vacation for a long time and I'd just broken up with Matt. She wanted me to check out several hotels in the area and give them feedback. They send a lot of ski-tour groups to Austria.

"On the day of the avalanche, I'd taken the train on a side trip to see some of the villages. While I was in Imst, I stopped at the hotel to check it out and wait for the storm to pass." She paused for a minute. "You know the rest."

He watched her through veiled eyes. "While you were waiting, I'd just left my father's room. He felt like a nap, so I decided I'd walk around the village to stretch my legs. After grabbing my jacket from my room, I headed for the stairs to go down to the lobby.

"Before I had a chance to put the jacket on, it felt like a bomb had gone off in the hotel. The next thing I knew, I was trapped in the darkness. I heard someone moaning and was grateful I wasn't alone. That person turned out to be *you*. The chances of our coming together on that day, at the moment, are astronomical, Sami."

"I know."

"It seems I have your sister to thank for our baby's existence. Have you told her you found Alberto Degenoli?"

She broke eye contact. "Yes. I was on the phone with her before I came in to breakfast."

"What was her reaction?"

Sami's head reared. "What you'd expect. Shock and shock."

"Did you tell her everything?"

"Yes."

"And of course she doesn't approve of you being here with me."

"No, but she's a mother, too, and knows Bruce loves their children desperately. In that regard she understands you and I are in a very precarious situation with no precedent."

"So she didn't give you advice?"

"No."

"I like her already."

"You'd love her. She's selfless…like you."

"Before you give me credit, remember I have yet to tell Eliana anything. My own siblings would call me a selfish swine for putting off the inevitable while I enjoy my son in private."

"They aren't in your shoes. I understand that now." After fighting him about coming here, her defense of him came as a gratifying surprise to him. She looked around them. "Why are all those boats out there?"

"People are scuba diving. Below them is the wreck of *Dhimitrios*. This is a popular area of the island."

She eyed him curiously. "Do you dive?"

"I did a lot in my youth. What about you?"

"No scuba. I've done some snorkeling and surfing in the summer in Carmel, but Matt's the expert."

Matt again. "Why don't we take a dip? Mara and Daimon will watch Ric. You'll find a locker below with all the swim gear including my sister, Claudia's, wetsuit if you need one. There should be flippers in there, too."

"Does your fiancée dive?"

"No. She's a horsewoman at heart. When I can get away, we go riding on their estate, but I must admit I prefer water sports. What about you?"

"I'm a jack of all trades, but excel at none."

"None?"

"Maybe table tennis."

He squinted at her. "Let's find out what kind of a swimmer you are."

"You're on. I'll be up as soon as I change."

After she kissed the baby and went below, he walked back to talk to his staff, who were clearly delighted to have charge of Ric for a while. Sami resurfaced faster than he would have supposed, wearing a wetsuit that hugged her body, revealing the lines and curves he'd memorized long ago. Desire for her overwhelmed him.

She sat on the end of the bench to put on the flippers. Trying to look at anything but her shapely legs was an impossibility. "I'm ready whenever you are."

Excited, Ric discarded his T-shirt. "Let's go." He helped her over to the side of the boat so she could jump in. He went in behind her. When her wet head appeared, he thought he'd never seen anyone so naturally alluring.

"We'll swim to that big rock. It's not far, but if you get tired, let me know and Daimon will bring the boat along. The sea gets rougher there."

Sami was glad they'd started swimming. In the boat she'd noticed his long powerful legs stretched out in front of him while they'd talked. The gorgeous sight of him almost made her lose her train of thought.

He paced his strokes so they stayed abreast of each other. The flippers gave her the momentum she needed to keep up. The closer they got to the rock, the bigger the swells became. When they were quite near, she could appreciate the beauty of the setting sun against the stunning blue of the sea.

Ric reached the rock first and caught her hand to pull her in so she could cling to it. "What is this place?" She was a little out of breath, but that had a lot to do with him being shirtless. His well-developed body made her mouth go dry. She'd had the same reaction when they'd been trapped. Without seeing him, she'd felt him and knew he was exceptional in many ways.

"The Goddess Aphrodite's birthplace. She was born out of the foam breaking on this rock. If you wore your blond hair long and flowing, you'd personify my own image of her."

Even though her heart was thudding, she laughed and threw her head back. "Oh—you Italian men are priceless."

"I'm half Cypriot," he declared, "raised on the stories of Zeus. Afraid her beauty would create jealousy among the other gods and cause war, he married her to Hephaestus."

Her smile deepened. "I know that story, too. But to his chagrin she was unfaithful to her husband and had many lovers."

One of them was the young god Adonis. With his wavy black hair and olive skin warmed by the sun, Ric could be a more adult version of him. However, she'd never seen Adonis depicted with hair on his chest. She decided she didn't dare tell Ric her thoughts to his face. He was engaged to be married. *Remember?*

"She had many children as a result," Ric teased.

A chuckle broke from her. "I've just had one. I'm afraid he's all I can handle."

Ric's black eyes grew shuttered. "Our baby's so perfect, he would make the gods jealous." The tone of his voice gave her gooseflesh.

"Then let's be thankful Zeus doesn't exist." It was frightening enough that Eliana didn't know about the baby. Sami feared her reaction when confronted with Ric's child.

Sami shouldn't be out here alone with him like this. Much too aware of him, she looked around her, noticing the pebbled beach in the distance. "It's all so natural here. Nothing's spoiled it."

"Perhaps not right now, but later you'll see tourists come here to the café above the beach. They believe these waters have mystical powers to soothe the troubled soul. You'll notice them clustering in the evenings to watch the sunset. That's the beauty of arriving by boat. When we want, we can slip back out to sea away from everyone else to witness the sun falling into the sea."

She believed that growing up in these waters had cultivated a poetic side to him. "Are you telling me you're a loner?"

"Sometimes. With the right person, you don't need anyone else," he said in a remote tone.

He'd said he wasn't in love with his fiancée. Maybe he was missing some woman from his past who'd been important to him. Sami had no idea. "Thank you for bringing me to this famous spot. How lucky am I? When I came to Italy, I couldn't have conceived of being at Aphrodite's birthplace two days later."

"Then you can imagine my incredulity that the woman I was trapped with is holding on to this rock with me."

She averted her eyes. "I think we ought to get back to the boat. Even if Ric is fine, I don't want Mara and Daimon worrying about us being gone so long."

"Never fear. My bodyguards are keeping watch."

"From where?" she asked in surprise.

"The shore and that sailboat out there."

Sami hadn't really noticed. Ric's masculine presence dominated everything. "They're very unobtrusive. It must be hard to watch you when you're having fun. I hope you pay them a good salary."

His laughter filled the sea air, mesmerizing her. Their gazes met in shared amusement. "I can't wait to tell them what you said."

She felt her cheeks grow warm. "Are they the same ones you told to follow me from the police station?"

"I'm not sure. They trade off shifts."

"Do you think they're scandalized to see you with someone other than Eliana?"

"Maybe. The only thing important is that they've been told that Ric is our son. They're too busy guarding us with their lives to do much else."

Though the sun was shining, she felt a dark shadow pass over her. "Have you had many threats on your life, Ric?"

"Enough to warrant protection, but I don't want you worrying about it."

"I'm not. I felt perfectly safe with you in the avalanche and feel the same way now."

"I'm relieved to hear it. Shall we go?"

"I'm ready."

"I'll race you back to the boat."

Her brows lifted. "Since you fly through the water like that striped dolphin you pointed out on the way here, what chance do I have?"

His lips twitched. "Those flippers give you an edge."

"Hmm. We'll see." Filled with adrenaline from being this close to him, she shoved off, determined to give him a run for his money even if the water was more difficult to handle. She thought she was doing fine until three-quarters of the way, when she lost power. Weakness had taken over.

Ric took one look and told her to get on his back. "Hold tight to my shoulders."

She obeyed him and let him do all the work. The sensation of swishing through the water on top of him gave her another kind of adrenaline rush. When they reached the ladder to the boat, she let go of him, afraid for him to know how much she'd enjoyed the ride. She'd never thought to be that close to him again.

He turned around. The motion tangled their legs. She let out a tiny gasp.

"Are you all right, Sami?"

"I—I'm fine." What a great liar she'd become.

"I'll remove your flippers so you can climb in."

No... She didn't want him touching her, but it was too late. He worked too fast. Like lightning he eased them off and tossed them in the boat. With no more impediments, Sami was able to heave herself up the rungs. Ric was right behind her. Their limbs brushed as they both got in.

Daimon was there to hand her a towel. "Welcome back. Did you enjoy it?"

"Yes, thank you. It was a wonderful trip, but before I do it again, I need to get in some conditioning. Poor Ric had to save me at the end." It was nothing new. He'd saved her eleven months ago.

"Surely you realize that was no penance?" he whispered near her ear before he headed for the front of the boat to check on their son. She felt the warmth of his breath against her skin in every atom of her body before following him.

Mara sat beneath the roof feeding the baby. She smiled at both of them. "He's been an angel. I hoped you would stay out longer."

"Please keep doing what you're doing. I'm going to run downstairs to shower and change."

"Take all the time you want."

What heaven to have a babysitter like Mara, but Sami didn't dare get used to such luxury.

Once she was out of her wet things, the warm shower felt good. She washed her hair. Afterward she put her jeans and top back on and walked out of the bathroom with a towel. As she started to dry her hair, a pair of strong hands took over.

She'd thought Ric would have stayed upstairs by the baby.

No man had ever dried her hair before. With Ric, she'd experienced all the wondrous aspects of being a woman. She was loving this too much. When she couldn't bear his touch any longer because she wanted more, she took a step back and pulled the towel from his hands. Unable to look him in the eye she said, "Thank you. I can manage now."

He was blocking the way. She suspected it was on purpose. "You were fantastic out swimming," he said in his deep voice. "After having little chance to swim since giving birth to our son, you're in amazing shape. That's no swimming pool out there. I'm impressed."

Sami needed to lighten the moment before she threw herself into his arms. She smoothed the hair out of her eyes. Being by the water had made it curlier. "I think I'm impressed, too." Or at least she had been until her energy had run out.

"I've enjoyed today, Signorina Argyle."

"The feeling's mutual."

"When you're ready, join me in the galley and we'll fix dinner for all of us."

She flicked him a glance. "You like to cook?"

"It's in my blood."

"I thought it was filled with seawater," she quipped.

"It's all part of the same thing." He kissed the end of her nose. "When we've dined to our heart's content, we'll pull up anchor and head back."

CHAPTER FIVE

AFTER eating a Greek smorgasbord of his favorite foods, Ric felt replete and glanced at the baby in his carrycot. He'd finally fallen asleep. Just he and Sami were on deck to watch the sunset. The other two had gone below. The evening was idyllic.

"Sami? I'm curious about something. If you hadn't traveled to Innsbruck, do you think you would have changed your mind about Matt?" The possibility that those two could still get together had been troubling him to the point he had to ask her about it.

"No."

"Yet since the avalanche you've left a door open for him."

She sighed. "Learning of my pregnancy, I realized another little person was going to be totally dependent on me. When I was young, my parents were taken from me. I was sad my baby would also be deprived of a father, so I determined I would be there for my son or daughter every minute.

"But Matt's a great guy and I have no doubts he'd be a great father. Maybe in time I could learn to love him as I should. I'm sure you know what that's like. But if we married, I'm worried he would feel he comes in second best with me because of the baby. That wouldn't be fair to him. He deserves to start out marriage with a woman who doesn't have a history like mine. *No one* has a history like ours, Ric," she half moaned. Her face closed up.

"Maybe I'll change my mind later and get in touch with him. But by then he might have found someone else. I just don't know. For a while longer at least, I've got to find my own way."

Hearing those words, Ric felt as if someone had just walked over his grave. His dream of a week alone with her and the baby had just gone up in smoke. What they were dealing with was too heavy, too serious, for him to live in denial any longer.

"So do I," he ground out. "The air's getting cooler. It's time to go home."

He hoped she would beg him to stay out longer, but she said nothing. With his gut churning, he pressed the button that pulled up the anchor and they headed back to the villa without further conversation.

Eventually they reached the point. By this time Daimon and Mara had come up on deck. As Ric pulled up to the dock, Daimon jumped out to secure the boat with the ropes. Ric helped him. Still hunkered on the pier, he looked down at Sami. She was busy removing the baby's life preserver.

"I've made a decision, Sami." She glanced up at him nervously. "Eliana's waiting for me to call her, but I need your input first before I make that call, because whatever happens from here on out, we're in this together."

Her expression sobered. "In what way?"

"Shall we fly back to Genoa in the morning? Once we're settled in the palazzo, I'll bring her over to meet you and Ric. Or, I can tell her to board her family's jet and fly down here tomorrow afternoon. Which option do you prefer?"

She handed him the baby before climbing onto the pier with the diaper bag. "I'm thankful you've decided to tell her. It's the right thing to do. I think we should face her here where there's no possibility of anyone else being around. As your future wife, she deserves every consideration we can give her. This is going to be very painful for her."

"I agree." Sami's courage and decency made her a remarkable woman.

"She'll be Ric's stepmother," she added. He heard the quiver in her voice. It reached deep inside him. "If it's possible, I want to be friends with her. But I realize that will take time considering the shock she's going to receive."

With those comments he'd just discovered Sami had a goodness in her not found in most people. For their baby to have a mother like her thrilled and humbled him.

"So be it. I'll call her when we go inside and tell her I want her to join me tomorrow evening. I won't indicate the reason until I pick her up at the airport. Until then, I'd like us to enjoy our vacation as long as possible. You'd like to spend time out by the swimming pool tomorrow, wouldn't you, *piccolo?*"

Ric clutched the baby to him, recognizing he only had another twenty-four hours before everything changed.

Sami headed for the villa and went up the stairs to the bedroom where she put the baby down. Ric followed. The baby had fallen fast asleep. After she covered him with a light blanket, she started to rise up and found herself too close to Ric. Instead of moving out of her way, he lifted his hands to her shoulders and kneaded them with increasing restlessness.

His eyes, so black and alive, devoured her features. "If you and I had been taken to the same hospital after the avalanche, we would have been able to get to know each other in the light and hold each other while we thanked providence our lives had been spared. Instead, it's taken all this time for us to finally meet. This is long overdue. After spending today with you, I need to hold you for a minute, Sami, so don't fight me."

He pulled her in to him, not giving her time to answer. The second he buried his face in her hair, she felt his hands rove over her back. Sami moaned and instinctively moved closer to his hard-muscled body. The feel of him, the enticing male scent of him, all were too familiar. The way he touched her and kissed the side of her neck brought déjà vu, sending a river of molten heat through her body. His touch had the power to turn her insides to liquid.

This was like before. She'd could hardly get enough

air then, and she had the same problem now, but not because of being enclosed by tons of snow. This time there was room to stand, and the fragrant air from the flowers growing outside moved through the windows and alcoves of the villa. Once again he'd intoxicated her, filling her with rapture that made her senses spiral and silenced her conscience.

"You're the most naturally beautiful woman I've ever known, Sami. I want you even more than before," he cried urgently before his mouth sought hers in a frenzy of need neither of them could control.

She didn't remember being carried to the bed. Somehow she was there with him, responding to her growing desire for this man who was thrilling her senseless. Every kiss created pure ecstasy. She felt herself going under, deeper and deeper.

"Since the avalanche, I've dreamed about us so many times. To think you're alive... *Sami*—"

"I know." She half sobbed the words. "I can't believe it either." She kissed the scar where the beam had hit his forehead. But in the act of doing it, she was suddenly seized by a cognizance of what was happening here.

When Ric would have found her mouth again, she rolled away from him and got to her feet, just far enough away that he couldn't reach her. She lost her balance and grabbed on to the end of the dresser.

"Don't do this to us. Come back here," he begged. His eyes were smoldering black fires.

She was one trembling mass of desire. "You think I don't want to? But we can't just do what we want, Ric.

It's clear you and I feel an attraction because of what happened during the avalanche and the miracle of meeting up again. But that's all this is. So far we've done nothing to be ashamed of. That's why this has to stop here and now, and never happen again."

He got up from the bed. She thought him even more gorgeous with his black hair disheveled. "So what are you saying?" he said in a voice of ice.

She backed away from him. "I'm saying that in Austria you and I were like two colliding heavenly bodies out in space. But those bodies have long since orbited away from each other despite the pull we've felt today. I suppose it's understandable since we both thought the other was dead."

He folded his arms. "So now that we've discovered we're amazingly alive, what about the next time we see each other and feel the pull?"

Sami took a shaky breath. "We'll deal with it. We *have* to. Yes, we shared one amazing connection together in the avalanche, but it wasn't real life. You have a whole new married life about to unfold. I have my studies."

When he didn't respond, she added, "In January I'm going to get on with my school work. I need a good career to be able to provide for me and Ric."

A tiny pulse throbbed at his temple where he'd been injured. "Where exactly?"

"At the University of Reno. I transferred my credits there when I left California. The nice thing is, the computer engineering department has a program that lets you go to school at night, so I'll be with Ric during the day. I've already arranged for several babysitters who've agreed to trade off helping me nights. It will all work out.

"As for you, you'll be married in a few weeks. After you and Eliana talk things over tomorrow evening, the three of us will sit down and work out a mutually beneficial visitation arrangement for our son. I'm praying that if she's a part of it, then she'll be more accepting of the situation."

Ric moved closer. "You think it's all going to be that simple?" he asked in a dangerously silky voice.

"No," she said, still looking at him. "Do you have a better solution? If so, I'm willing to hear it. But not tonight. I'm really tired after my swim. We all need a good night's sleep."

Stillness surrounded him. "If you should want me for any reason, I'll be in my study downstairs making a phone call."

Please leave now and get it over with. Sami's willpower was nonexistent.

Ric must have heard her plea. In the next instant he was gone.

Sami slept in late. When she came downstairs the next morning, she discovered Mara had served breakfast out on the patio surrounding the pool. There was no sign of Ric or the baby, but his carrycot was there. As she sat down to eat, Ric came through the alcove holding her little darling. Their eyes met.

"Good morning. I'm sorry I got up so late."

He walked over so she could kiss the baby. "That's the

idea when you're on vacation. It gave Ric and me a chance to go for a walk and have a talk together, man to man."

She smiled. "Did you two set the world straight?"

"Of course." He reciprocated with a heart-melting smile of his own.

On the surface, you wouldn't think they had a care, but Sami couldn't take the invisible tension she was feeling any longer. She needed an answer to one burning question. "Were you able to reach Eliana last night?"

He nodded without noticeable emotion. "She'll be arriving at six-thirty this evening."

"I realize she doesn't suspect anything. That makes me nervous."

"If it will ease your anxiety, I did tell her I had something of great importance I needed to talk to her about. It put her on the alert, which was good." He expelled a deep breath. "If there were someone to blame in this… but there isn't." His voice trailed. "You and I clung to life until the last breath. If that was a sin, then so be it, but I won't allow our son to suffer because of it."

"I believe you."

Sami didn't know how she was going to stand meeting Eliana, but she had to go through with it. No doubt Ric's fiancée was an outstanding woman, otherwise he wouldn't be marrying her. But tonight when he would introduce them and they would look at each other, Eliana's eyes would be staring at the woman Ric had made love to in the dark with the result of pregnancy.

Could Sami expect to see any understanding, or would bitter resentment always cloud the other woman's vision?

She looked up at the powder-blue sky. The weather had warmed up to seventy degrees at the pool and was almost balmy. With such brilliant blue water beyond the point, it was hard to believe it was December.

Sami cast a covert glance at Ric, who'd gone over to lie down on one of the sun loungers to play with the baby. He'd dressed in a wine-colored polo and white cargo pants. His well-honed body made it difficult to look anywhere else.

Another sigh escaped. She could only imagine what was going through his mind right now. Once he told Eliana the truth, the word would be out. It wasn't just his fiancée he would have to placate. His family and hers, their friends, everyone who knew and loved him would have questions he would have to answer.

What made this so hard was to realize that a very private act between the two of them—an act even *they* had trouble explaining—would become public knowledge. Because of Ric's prominence, both he and Sami would be the targets of gossip, in some cases malicious. She would hate the notoriety, but she and the baby would be back in Reno where she wouldn't have to be around the paparazzi on a twenty-four-hour basis. Ric would bear the brunt of it.

Of course he'd handle it, but his marriage would suffer. And though she knew he'd go to the greatest lengths to protect their son from being hurt when he was on visitation, it was inevitable the baby would feel it and have to live with it growing up.

Her desire to lift Ric's spirits until Eliana arrived

prompted Sami to get up from the table. "Excuse me for a minute. I'll be right back."

"Hurry. We like your company."

His little personal asides made mincemeat of her emotions. She dashed through the villa and up the stairs for his gift. She'd started making it for his father after finding out she was pregnant. Little did she dream she would be giving it to Ric himself.

Formula wasn't the only thing at the bottom of her suitcase. She opened the lid and pulled out the scrapbook which she'd wrapped in Christmas paper ahead of time. Hugging it to her chest, she hurried back downstairs to the pool.

He was so preoccupied with the baby, he didn't see her coming. "Merry Christmas again, Ric," she called to him, announcing her presence.

He looked up in time for her to hand it to him. "I brought this to give your father for Christmas. I've decided now would be the best time for you to have it."

While he sat up to open it, she picked up the baby and stood there to watch him leaf through the pages.

Sami had put everything in there: pictures of her, her grandparents, more pictures of her sister's family and their parents, the apartment in Reno, the picture the hospital had taken of Ric right after he was born, cards from friends, comments from the pediatrician, more pictures of him turning one week, then two, then three, his room, his crib and baby toys. Everything she could think of to preserve memories for his grandfather.

"Those three photos are the ultrasound pictures. Can

you believe that's our little Ric there? The technician said he had a strong heartbeat and everything looked normal. You'll never know my relief."

Ric went so quiet, she wondered if something was wrong. Then he looked up with those jet-black eyes suspiciously bright. "I'll cherish this forever, Sami." She hardly recognized his voice it was so husky.

Thrilled with his response she said, "When you told me you'd missed the first two months of his life and didn't want to miss any more, I was doubly glad I made this. While you enjoy it, I'm going to put this little guy to bed for a nap."

"Wait— Stay right where you are." He got up from the lounger and dashed into the villa. Not a minute later and he came back outside with Daimon.

"He's going to take a picture of us with my cell phone," Ric explained. In the next breath he came to stand next to Sami and put his arm around her shoulders, pulling her close enough to set off a burst of adrenaline.

"This one's for posterity and will go in the last page of the book. Take a dozen pictures, Daimon. Then we want to take pictures of you and Mara holding him. Before long I intend to fill up a whole new scrapbook with memories."

But when, Ric? Here on the island isn't real life.

After all the picture-taking was done, they went upstairs to put the baby down, then tiptoed out of the room. Sami assumed Ric would use this free time to do the business he'd come to Paphos to accomplish. Nothing could have surprised her more than when he told her he wanted her to drive to town with him.

"I've arranged for Mara to watch the baby while we're gone. I want to show you around the ancient part of the city."

"What about your work?"

"It's getting done."

When? In the middle of the night? How did he do it and still get up with the baby?

"If you feel you have time, I'd love to do some sight-seeing." As long as she could be with him, she honestly didn't care what they did. She was storing up memories before she had to go back home.

"The weather's warm enough to go without a coat, but if you want one, I'll wait for you downstairs."

"I'm fine the way I am."

When his eyes smiled like that, she felt complete. "Then let's make the most of the time."

Within minutes they were driving on the A-6 toward the city they'd passed on the cruiser yesterday. He gave her a running commentary about the origins of the sprawling modern coastal town of 47,000 people.

Once in the busy part of the new Paphos, Ric stopped to buy a stroller for the baby. "We'll need one. It'll be nice to push him around whether we're out walking around or at the villa."

Sami saw a clothing shop and popped in to buy an extra couple of outfits for herself. Everything was decked out for Christmas. Nearby Ric found a sweets shop that sold drinks and *loukoumades*. He bought a sack of the delicious donut balls with syrup for them to eat along the way. "My friends and I used to stuff ourselves with these."

"I can see why. I can't stop with just one."

They drove on. No one was more fun than Ric when he was lighthearted. She became the pushover who went along with all his ideas because she couldn't help herself.

"Ahead of us is Palaepaphos, the old city. It was the island's capital in Greco-Roman times and the main focal point of Aphrodite-worship for the entire Aegean. I'm taking you to see some outstanding mosaics that still remain in the Roman governor's palace."

For the next two hours they explored the remains of everything from villas, palaces and theaters to fortresses and tombs. "Oh, Ric, this is all so incredible."

"Isn't it? I spent all my holidays here, pretending it was my secret world. Come on. I want to show you one more thing before we go back."

Sami dreaded the fact that this time with Ric was almost over. Nothing would be the same after Eliana arrived. If it were in her power, she'd make this time with him last forever.

They soon came to a jewel of an ancient church. "This is the Agia Kyriaki Chrysopolitissa parish church, one of my favorite places. My mother loved it and always brought us here."

"Is it still operational?"

"Yes. They even hold English mass."

She loved its architecture. "There's a very spiritual aspect about the whole place."

His dark eyes fastened on hers. "This city was blessed when Paul of Tarsus visited here in the first century A.D."

Sami reflected on Ric's upbringing. "You were blessed to have a mom you loved so much raise you."

He moved closer to her. "Now you understand why I'm full of gratitude for the way you love our son. Your grandparents did a wonderful job with you."

"Pat and I weren't the easiest children. They'll get a crown in heaven, that's for sure."

While she was caught up with so many feelings she didn't dare express, she was conscious of a clock ticking away. "I think Mara will wonder if we're ever coming back."

Ric's mouth turned up in a half smile. "She hopes we won't."

They started for the car. "Do she and Daimon have children?"

"Yes. Both their married daughters live in Nicosia. They visit back and forth with the grandchildren on a regular basis."

"That makes me happy to hear it." She glanced at her watch and couldn't believe how long they'd been gone. "It's almost time for Eliana's plane to arrive. We need to hurry home."

"Relax. We'll make it."

Ric seemed in no rush. Sami tried to heed his advice, but she was too restless. When they reached the villa, she hurried inside to find the baby. Holding him always calmed her down.

Mara had put him in the carrycot while she was in

the kitchen cooking. Sami entered with Ric to find their son lying there open-eyed and perfectly content until Ric hunkered down to talk to him. The second he saw his daddy, he started crying, wanting to be held. On cue, Ric was right there to pick him up and nestle him against his chest.

Sami burst into laughter. "What a little faker he is. I swear that happens every time with you."

A smile lit up Mara's face. "He knows his *papa*."

"Unfortunately his *papa* needs to get ready to leave for the airport," Sami said. Her gaze shot to Ric. "I'll take him so you won't be late."

She felt his hesitation before he handed the baby over.

"At least Ric still acts happy to come to me. I'd begun to fear he might have forgotten me because of his new infatuation with you."

"Sami..."

Afraid to look in Ric's eyes she said, "I'm taking this young man upstairs. Thanks for everything, Mara."

"My pleasure. He won't need a bottle for a while. I think he's getting sleepy."

"All right then. Let's go change you."

Ten minutes later he'd fallen to sleep. As Sami turned to go take her shower, Ric made an appearance. He looked too gorgeous in a silky charcoal dress shirt and black trousers she hadn't seen before. Her heart pounded outrageously.

"I wanted you to know I'm leaving now."

"I—I'll see you later then." She stumbled over the

words. Fear for what was going to happen had chilled her blood. "I'll pray things go well."

Without saying anything, he went over to the crib and rubbed their little boy's head. "I'll be back, *tesoro mio,*" he whispered.

"What did you just call him?"

"My treasure." His gaze swerved to hers. "When you came to find my father, you brought me the world, Sami."

His words liquefied her insides. "He's my whole world, too." She struggled to keep her voice steady. "Do you have any advice for me for when I meet Eliana?"

A brooding look stole over his handsome face. "Simply be yourself."

That didn't help her. "How old is she?"

"Twenty-five."

A year younger than Sami. "Have you—" She stopped herself, needing to bite her tongue out.

"Have we been intimate?"

"It's none of my business."

"The answer is yes."

Sami had no right to feel wounded by the admission, but she did. Horribly. But she was glad she knew. It put things into perspective. He was a man with a man's appetite and Eliana was his fiancée, after all. Women always dramatized everything.

Well, Sami refused to be like that. Everyone knew that the majority of couples, engaged or not, didn't wait for marriage to sleep together. The fact that Sami hadn't been intimate with a man except Ric put her in that tiny minority.

He darted her a quick glance. "I'll answer the next question you haven't asked yet. I've enjoyed my share of women over the years."

"If Eliana knows that, then perhaps she won't be as hurt when you tell her about us."

His lids drooped over his eyes. "That's a nice thought. Let's hang on to it, shall we?"

"Ric—"

"I should be back with her within forty-five minutes."

Her body trembled. "I'll be ready. What shall I wear?"

He scrutinized her from her hair to her sandaled feet. "You're breathtaking with or without clothes. Put on whatever feels the most comfortable."

After Ric had left the bedroom, Sami stood in the shower paralyzed by what he'd said. How could he reduce everything to its most intimate and personal when he was preparing to pick up his soon-to-be wife at the airport?

Yet, on the heels of that thought, she had to remember he'd been intimate with both Sami and Eliana. The situation didn't fit any scenario she knew of.

Coming to the island had been a mistake. They'd gotten into a false sense of vacation mode. Last night things had almost spiraled out of control. Because of the baby, she assumed that was the reason they'd both subconsciously let down their guard. But one thing was certain. She refused to put herself into such a vulnerable position again.

The only thing to do was get through the next few hours while they all talked, then she'd fly home in the morning. She'd done her part so Ric could enjoy the baby, but now it was over. It didn't matter if he wanted their son with him all the time. That wouldn't be possible. Reno and Genoa were thousands of miles apart. After his marriage and honeymoon, they could talk on the phone and plan how to arrange visitation.

While her mind pored over how she would tell him she was leaving, she did her hair and makeup. After that she opened the closet door and put on her navy blue suit, matching it with a lighter blue silk blouse. The rest of the clothes she'd brought with her comprised a few casual jeans and tops. Sami wanted to look her best. Nothing but the suit was dressy enough for this first meeting with a princess, no matter how casual the surroundings.

When she was ready, she went downstairs and asked Mara to listen for the baby while she walked out to the private marina to take in the view. She hoped Ric and Eliana would arrive while she was away from the villa. Ric could show her the baby before she had to face Sami.

Mara acted delighted and offered to feed him if he awakened. Sami thanked her and stepped outside.

The sun had set an hour ago. Sami presumed Ric would be back fairly soon. Twilight had come on fast and the air was cooler, yet she glimpsed sailboats and cruisers out enjoying the evening. From the corner of her eye she saw a jet climbing in the sky from Paphos airport. Under the right circumstances this time of night could be magical, but all Sami experienced was a heavy heart.

She walked along the path bordering the sand. Everyone knew weddings were for the bride. A bride had the right to expect that the days leading up to her wedding would be filled with excitement. It killed Sami to imagine that because she'd come to Genoa looking for Ric's grandfather, Eliana's excitement would now vanish as if it had never been.

Again Pat's predictions came floating back at her.

Neither Sami nor Ric could change things, but she would go out of her way to appease Eliana in any way she could in order not to do more damage. Lost in thought, she didn't realize she'd been out longer than she'd planned. It had grown dark. She retraced her steps back to the villa and met Daimon coming toward her.

"Enrico sent me to find you."

"I purposely stayed out to give him time to be with Eliana and the baby."

"They've been here awhile. He was worried about you."

"I'm sorry. Where are they?"

"In the living room by the fireplace."

Sami walked inside and made her way through to the front of the house. She peered around the corner to see the couple over on the couch. In the open-necked charcoal shirt and dark trousers, Ric had never looked more appealing. He'd nestled the baby against his shoulder. His little head bobbed, signaling he was awake. Both were heartbreakingly attractive.

Eliana was seated near him wearing a stunning watermelon-colored suit. She had class written all over her and could have been a model for the latest princess doll with her dark blond hair falling in curls over her shoulders.

CHAPTER SIX

"HELLO?" Sami called softly to announce her entrance.

At the sound of her voice, Ric's black eyes shot to hers and he sprang to his feet. The way he was looking at her underlined what Daimon had said about him being worried. She hadn't meant to alarm him.

Her gaze strayed to Eliana whose head had turned in her direction. Large amber eyes gave Sami a wintry stare of condemnation. Otherwise her classically Italian features were devoid of animation.

Little did Eliana know she didn't have anything to fear from Sami. But the baby was another matter, because Ric had claimed him. He loved their baby to the depth of his being and intended to be a hands-on father whenever possible.

At the moment his remote countenance was more pronounced than it had been when he'd told her the reason he'd gotten rid of his title. She groaned inwardly for him.

"Christine Argyle, please meet my fiancée, Princess Eliana Fortulezza."

Sami had known he was marrying nobility, but hearing his fiancée's title and seeing her in person at last still took some getting used to. "How do you do, Princess Fortulezza?"

Eliana rose to her feet. "Signorina Argyle," she said and they shook hands.

Ric's fiancée studied Sami without revealing any visible emotion. Though Ric had been honest about his reasons for marrying Eliana, no one could know what was in his fiancée's heart. She'd been trained to maintain her dignity, but now that this ghastly moment was upon them, Sami thought the other woman was awesome.

"Come on," Ric said. "We'll go into the dining room where we can sit around the table to talk." Sami followed them, noting Eliana's tall, slender figure and the three dazzling diamonds of her engagement ring.

The carrycot was still perched on the table. Ric put the baby down in it, then pulled out chairs for her and Eliana. Since her little boy seemed content, Sami sat down without kissing him. She didn't want to get him all worked up and create a fuss.

Mara came in to serve coffee and biscotti. Ric thanked her before she left them alone. His dark, solemn eyes slid to Sami. "I've told Eliana everything that happened last January."

Having said that much, the onus was now on Sami. She cleared her throat and eyed Eliana. "Then you realize that when I went to the police station two days ago, I was expecting, or at least hoping, to meet Ric's father."

"Yes."

This was so painful for Sami, she could only imagine how shocked and hurt Eliana had to be. "I can't tell you how sorry I am to have caused you this kind of grief. I had no idea the elder Mr. Degenoli had died, or that Ric had survived the avalanche." Her voice faltered. "When he lost consciousness, I thought he was dead. Neither of us dreamed we would ever leave our tomb alive."

"So Enrico explained. Did he tell you to call him Ric?" she asked in heavily accented English.

Out of all the questions she might have asked, that was the last one Sami would have expected. "When I realized I wasn't alone in the dark, I asked who was there. He said he was Ric Degenoli. I was thankful he spoke English and told him my name was Sami."

"Sami?"

"My father's name was Samuel. That's how I got the nickname." She leaned forward. "Eliana—please believe me. I have absolutely no intention of ruining your life. I know you're going to be married on New Year's Day. Tomorrow morning I'm taking the baby back to Reno with me."

She purposely didn't look at Ric while she spoke to Eliana. "Once the wedding and honeymoon are over and you've settled into married life, then visitation can be discussed. But be assured my life is in America."

The other woman studied her for a minute. "Enrico tells me there's a man who wishes to marry you."

Sami couldn't fault Ric for telling his fiancée everything. The whole truth and nothing but. No doubt it would make things more bearable for Eliana if Sami were to say that she and Matt would be getting married shortly. But she couldn't, because it would never happen. Sami didn't love Matt with all her heart and soul. In the past twenty-four hours, she'd had that confirmed beyond any lingering doubt.

"There is, but I've decided against marrying him." Her announcement caused something to flare in the recesses of Ric's eyes, whether surprise because she'd been so frank about it, Sami couldn't tell. Eliana didn't flinch. "Perhaps if I give you a little background, you'll understand.

"I was young when my parents died. Though I adored my grandparents, I ached for a mother and father. When Ric was born I made a vow. Since he would never know his father in this life, I would devote my life to raising my precious son to the very best of my ability.

"For the last two months I've thought of nothing else and don't see another man giving my baby the love he'll need." Watching Ric in action with their child had settled the question for her once and for all. Anyone other than his own father wouldn't do.

"How will you live?"

Sami had half expected Eliana's practical question. Ric's fiancée could be forgiven for thinking Sami was out for everything she could get from him. It was time to reassure her on that point.

"Did Ric mention to you that I was in graduate school before I flew to Austria?"

"He said something about it."

"I intend to go back to it. Being a computer engineer will provide me with a good living to help me take care of the two of us and pay back my loans."

"How in debt are you?"

Again Sami understood why she was curious. "By the time I've received my master's degree, I'll probably owe at least $40,000, but I'll pay it back slowly after I'm employed. I'm fortunate to go to a university where I can be with the baby all day and attend classes at night.

"Once I'm back there, I'll email you my schedule. We'll work things out so Ric gets to see his son when it's convenient for you. Do you have any other questions you want to ask me?"

After a few seconds she said, "No."

Then there was nothing more to talk about. Good. Sami couldn't sit here any longer. If Eliana was struggling to hold it all together, she didn't give anything away.

Sami stood up without having tasted her coffee. "If you'll excuse me, I need to put the baby down and go to bed." She went around to lift him from his carrycot. On her way out of the room, she paused for a moment. "I'm glad Ric brought you here tonight so we could meet, Eliana. I wish you two every happiness on your forthcoming marriage."

Even though Eliana and Ric hadn't been engaged last January, Sami had the conviction that the strange circumstances surrounding the baby's conception had driven a wedge that could never be closed. "Since I know you have a lot to discuss, I'll say good-night."

Eliana looked relieved. So was Sami, who hurried to the bedroom, thankful the dreaded meeting was over. Once inside, she hurried upstairs and put the baby down long enough to change and slip into her robe. After that she bathed him and gave him his bottle, needing to feel him close to her.

She still shivered from the look on Ric's face before she'd rushed out of the dining room. It said she hadn't had the last word when it came to her going back to the States. But despite how crazy he was about their baby, he had to face reality. The only way to relieve the tension was for Sami to go home.

As soon as her little cherub had fallen asleep, she put him down in the crib. Afraid she'd toss and turn in agony all night, she took a sleeping pill and turned off her lamp before climbing into bed.

If the drug worked and she fell into a deep enough sleep, she knew Ric would get up in the night with the baby. The experience would give Eliana a taste of what it would be like when it was their turn to take care of him.

While she lay there waiting for needed oblivion, her mind went over the scene in the living room. Sami had given out enough information for Eliana to put her own spin on it. No doubt she believed Sami had come to Italy hoping Ric's father would fund her graduate-school costs. When she'd found Ric alive, that was even better. The count was worth a fortune and would do anything for his son. He'd already proved it.

Surely by now it had entered Eliana's mind that a lesser man with his kind of money could have paid Sami off and been done with the problem without any knowledge of it coming to light. *Not Ric.* He not only loved the idea of being a father, he genuinely loved playing with the baby and seeing to all his needs. You couldn't fake that kind of caring.

Eliana had to be seeing a whole new side to her fiancé. It ought to reassure her he'd be a marvelous father to any children they would have one day. But Eliana would have to get past this obstacle before she could begin to appreciate how exceptional Ric really was.

Still in turmoil, Sami turned on her other side. For the three of them to meet and talk had been the only thing to do, but none of them had come out of it unscathed. Her gaze lit on the baby, who had no idea what was going on. Her sweet little baby… Hot tears trickled out the corners of her eyes.

When next Sami knew anything, she discovered it was after 10:00 a.m. That pill had eventually knocked her out. With her timing off, it meant she would have to hurry to arrange for an evening flight out of Paphos.

There was no sign of the baby. Ric and Eliana must have come in to take care of him. If not them, Mara. With her pulse racing, Sami quickly dressed in jeans and a blouse before hurrying downstairs. She expected to find him with Ric and Eliana in the breakfast room of the villa. Instead the housekeeper was the one to greet her.

"Good morning, Sami. Enrico is at the pool with the baby. I'll serve your breakfast out there."

"Thank you, Mara."

She rushed through the alcoves to reach the pool at the side of the villa. As he'd been yesterday, Ric was seated at the umbrella table, but this morning he was dressed in a pale blue suit and tie. Rather than reading the newspaper, he was playing with the baby, whose animated responses touched her heart. An empty baby bottle lay next to his coffee. Apparently Eliana wasn't up yet.

Ric saw her and got to his feet, the quintessential Genoan aristocrat. *Her baby's father.* Not in a hundred lifetimes could Sami have dreamed up this picture.

"I'm glad you're awake," he said as she approached. "We have to talk. Ric has been looking for you."

Sami leaned over their son. "I think your *papa* is just teasing me to make me feel better. You've been having a wonderful time, haven't you?" She caught his little hands and pressed kisses all over them and his face and neck. After she lifted her head, she turned to his father. "Is Eliana still in bed?"

His eyes roved over her features for a moment. "No. I just got back from driving her to the airport. She flew home in her father's company jet."

Sami's composure slipped. "I'm sick for her, Ric," she cried. "The news had to ruin her dreams. With your wedding so imminent, I don't know how she's handling it."

Lines marred his striking face. "She's not" came the grim admission. Sami's heart plummeted. Ric rubbed the back of his neck as she'd seen him do before. "There's much more to Eliana's reaction than even I had imagined."

"You're talking about the inevitable scandal," she whispered. "I know it will be awful, but compared to a little baby who needs a father and mother, surely she'll come to terms with this in time?"

The lines marring his features made him look older. "The baby plays a negligible part in what's happened."

Sami frowned. "What do you mean?"

"Early this morning I heard from my attorney. The title is now officially gone." His eyes narrowed to slits. "What you said in passing was prophetic. Knowing she'll no longer be addressed as Countess is what has destroyed Eliana's dream. She's demanding that I have it reinstated."

"Did you tell her that's impossible?"

"She doesn't understand the word. As for little Ric, she has no intention of being a stepmother to my child."

"She's saying that now because she wants her own children with you, Ric."

"Not if there isn't a title to bestow on our firstborn son. Her solution to the problem is unthinkable," his voice rasped, igniting her panic.

"What do you mean by that?"

"She won't consider visitation. Either I give up all rights to Ric and never see him again, or the wedding is off. She's giving me until Christmas Eve day to make a final decision. In the meantime she won't discuss this with anyone."

Sami swallowed hard. "She's not a parent yet, or she wouldn't have laid down those rules. Eliana doesn't mean what she said. It was her pain lashing out. You have to give her time. Though the pain's excruciating, in a few days she'll have recovered enough to think more clearly."

"No. She's thinking clearly now. Until last summer Eliana and I only knew each other socially and were never in any kind of relationship. What happened between you and me had no bearing on her, but now she's in a rage because I never told her about you. I explained that I'd gone looking for you and couldn't find you. For all I knew, you had died. Even if I'd found you, I wouldn't have dreamed I'd made you pregnant."

"I had to explain the same thing to Matt. When the doctor told me the reason why I hadn't been feeling well, I almost fainted and had to stay lying down for an hour before I could leave his office. He talked to me about diet and prenatal vitamins, but I hardly heard him for the shock I was in.

"If I hadn't become pregnant, none of it would have come out." Sami shook her head. "Eliana could have no idea how this situation has affected you and me, but it's so hard to explain."

"She doesn't want an explanation. All she cares about is the title."

"Ric—I have to believe that when the worst of her agony subsides, she'll realize she wants to be your wife under any circumstances."

"That's where you're wrong. You weren't raised a princess with specific expectations to be met."

Sami hugged her arms to her waist. "Do you think she's capable of understanding what it would mean for you to give up your parental rights to Ric?"

"She doesn't want to understand, because the baby isn't a factor."

"But he's your son!"

"Eliana grew up in her father's world of black and

white. His daughter is a product of that environment. When he hears about this, he'll demand I get the title back, because he puts his desires above everything else. He'll tell me to pay you off for the child I fathered by some freak accident."

She shuddered. "I've known all along no one would believe what happened to us."

"Certainly not Eliana. When I told her you were in Austria on a working vacation for your sister's travel agency, she's convinced you targeted me when you found out Count Degenoli was registered there. Employing your wiles, you ended up sleeping with me in the hotel before the avalanche struck, and decided to use the tragedy as an alibi to cover our flirtation."

Sami sank into the chair. "Actually I can't blame her for thinking that."

"Nor I. She assumes you came to Italy as soon as the baby could travel in order to extort money from me. Moreover she thinks I decided to rescind the title because you phoned me from Reno and told me about the pregnancy a long time ago.

"Because I was already engaged to her, she assumed I immediately made the necessary arrangements so I'd be able to legally claim Ric as my firstborn, thus cheating her."

"You can't fault her logic, Ric. I'm afraid everyone who learns about us will think the same thing. Do you think Eliana always hoped to marry you?"

"I have no idea." He came to a standstill, gripping the back of one of the dining-room chairs until his knuckles showed white. "Our fathers have brushed shoulders in the same business circles for years, but I didn't consider getting to know her until June of this year. In November I asked her to marry me and we set a date for the wedding."

"She's very lovely. Not very many women in her kind of pain would have handled our meeting with so much poise."

"Interestingly enough, she said the same thing about you."

Sami couldn't look at him. "Unfortunately if Eliana thinks you've lied to her about our first meeting, then she *does* see me as a menace. It wouldn't matter how many times I tell her I won't stand in the way of her happiness, she won't listen."

He cocked his dark head. "Perhaps deep down she does believe it. That's what bothers her more."

"Why do you say that?"

"Do I need to spell it out?" he fired. "Not every woman and man trapped in a situation like ours would have sought comfort as we did."

Again her body grew warm. "I know," she admitted reluctantly.

"I'm still haunted by those feelings and why we acted on them. I can assure you my life hasn't been the same since that experience."

"Neither has mine," she confessed in a tremulous voice. "Maybe it was because we believed our time had run out and we were both single and free at the time to act without hurting anyone else. But the same can't be said of us now."

"No," he murmured. "Since then, we have a marvelous child who needs his mother and father." Without warning he scooped up the baby, laughing triumphantly. The happy sound was a revelation. He alternated kissing and cuddling him close. Ric treated their son as if he'd always been in his life.

Her heart ran away with her. "But everything has changed—"

"I agree. We've all changed. Last night Eliana could feel a certain tension between you and me she couldn't cut through. Don't forget you kissed me back yesterday and the day before, Sami."

"I've forgotten nothing!" When he'd laid her down on the hotel bed in Genoa to talk, her body had come alive again without her volition. Yesterday they'd reached blindly for each other in the bedroom after putting Ric down. She'd only come to her senses at the last second.

He eyed her with a penetrating glance. "I'm glad to hear you say it, because you're not going back to Reno yet. Since you've flown this long way, the three of us are going to stay here and enjoy this time together while Eliana works this out in her mind.

"Maybe the impossible will happen and she'll decide she wants this marriage badly enough to compromise. It'll mean going up against her father, but she knows my terms. Without visitation, I won't marry her."

Sami couldn't stop shivering. "This is all so mean. She's been looking forward to her wedding day since you announced the engagement in November. To defy her father's wishes in order to keep you will be a hard thing, Ric. If she isn't able to go against him, then she'll be forced to call off the wedding and suffer the humiliation of having to undo all the arrangements of a huge public marriage like yours."

"That's where you're wrong, Sami. With my family still in mourning, we'd already planned our wedding to take place in the privacy of the palazzo chapel with only our families in attendance. No reporters will be allowed inside. The news will leak out, it always does, but there'll be no photo ops or press releases, no official reception."

"The poor thing." Tears filled her eyes. "Why didn't you fly back with her?"

"After you left us last night, I told her I'd take her back to Genoa in my own plane this morning and we'd talk to her parents together while you and the baby remained here. She agreed. But when we reached the airport this morning, she suddenly changed her mind and told me she needed to talk to her parents alone first."

That's why he was dressed in a suit. "Why do you think she didn't want you to be with her when she faced them? With you there explaining everything, how could they possibly doubt your honesty?"

"You want the truth?" he rapped out.

"Ric—if we don't have that, we don't have anything!"

"She assumes you and I have slept together since your arrival in Genoa. Last night she asked me not to touch her."

Sami moaned. "Does that mean—"

"It means she slept in the other guest bedroom," he answered.

She bit her lip. "Did she help you with the baby when you got up in the night to feed him?"

"If she heard me and Ric, she didn't make an appearance."

"Obviously she was in too much pain."

He exhaled sharply. "It's commendable how much credit you give her."

"I'm not the woman who has been looking forward to her marriage to you. She's crushed. In the face of what she's dealing with, I admire her more for her honesty, no matter hard it is on both of you."

Ric raked a hand through his black hair. "You're an extraordinary woman, Sami."

"No, I'm not—" she cried. "This is so awful for both of you. I have my own life to go back to, but you two have to wade through so much to make this work!" She buried her face in her hands. "Did you disabuse her about us?"

"In what regard?" he drawled.

"That nothing has happened between us since I came to Italy."

"I wouldn't say that," he countered in a tone that sent little darts of awareness through her body.

Exasperated she said, "You know what I mean."

"Just because you and I haven't ended up in bed yet doesn't rule out what goes on whenever we're near each other." Her trembling started up again. After a pause he added, "Even if I'd assured her we didn't pick up where we'd left off in January, do you imagine it would have done any good?"

Her shoulders slumped. "I should never have come."

"We've been over this ground before," he said in an iron-clad voice. "Don't ever say that again."

She took a deep breath to pull herself together. By acknowledging his son from the start, Ric hadn't given his fiancée a choice. Surely Eliana was aware of his strong will. He wouldn't capitulate. It was up to her to decide what she could handle. No doubt she wanted to scratch Sami's eyes out or worse.

"You need to fly back to Genoa where you'll be close if she wants to see you. I'll leave for Reno on the next plane out of Paphos."

"No. That you *won't* do. For the sake of propriety, she's already set down the condition that you and I stay away from the city until the twenty-fourth."

"Ric—tell me the truth. If she doesn't come around and there's no marriage, then what will it cost you besides the woman you asked to marry you? Don't insult me by pretending this won't shake your world."

He wore an implacable expression. "That's for me to worry about."

"But I *do* worry!" she declared. "My reappearance in your world has done irreparable damage. If anyone should go to her parents, *I* should. I'll ask my sister and her husband to come with me. They'll verify what we've told Eliana.

"If we can convince her parents that I wasn't out to extort anyone or try to break you up, then it's possible they'll forgive you for having a human weakness. Good heavens, they're parents and will have to understand you want to be able to see your son on a regular basis. If

Eliana is willing to accept the baby, then the marriage can still take place."

His smile wasn't reflected in his eyes. "Your reasoning is without fault, Sami. You'd make a very convincing courtroom lawyer. But the crux of the real problem lies in the loss of the title. Eliana has been imagining herself as Countess Degenoli."

"You honestly think she can't get over that?"

"Not her or her father," his voice grated. "She's conflicted at her foundation. It wouldn't matter if you and your family were there to plead my case and win over her parents. She has her own war to fight inside. As I told you earlier, I'm going to find out what's really important to her."

Ric was a wonderful man. A prize. All this time Sami had assumed Eliana had learned to love him more than life. But what if that wasn't perfectly true? What if she loved him with strings?

Since this was virtually an arranged marriage, it was obvious there was a voice inside Ric that had always entertained his doubts about her. He'd gotten rid of his title as soon as he could. Maybe it had been a test. When Sami had asked him if it was such a terrible burden, his answer had left her in no doubt.

While she stood there trying to analyze his psyche, he peeled off his suit jacket and loosened his tie, as if he couldn't wait to remove the shackles of society. "After I've changed, we'll take another boat ride, this time in the other direction."

"What if someone who knows you and Eliana sees us together with Ric?"

"If they do, it won't matter because the person who needed to know the truth was Eliana. By now she's talked to her parents on the phone. If I'm not mistaken, they've already laid out a strategy to deal with the gossip in case Eliana says she wants to end the engagement. Until then, that leaves you and me free to play. When the time comes for us to leave Cyprus, you'll have seen many of my favorite haunts."

Warning bells were going off. "You said you were here to work. If I go home, it will give you the time you need."

His body stiffened. "If you can give me one good reason why…" His voice snaked through to her insides.

"Even if Eliana has set up the rules for this intolerable situation, it's not right for us to be together like this while you're still engaged."

He moved closer to her. "I think the real reason goes deeper than that. You're afraid to be alone with me."

She clutched the baby tighter. "My greatest fear is that your fiancée will always consider me an immoral woman. I felt it without her having to say it. If she's willing to work out visitation so your marriage can go through, I don't want her to hate me forever. Otherwise it could reflect on little Ric.

"To be honest, it hurts me that she doesn't know the real me. For that matter, neither do you. These last few days haven't been an example of real life, Ric. We're still strangers with our own individual lives to lead once I'm gone."

The silence between them was tangible. Finally he spoke. "Then let me get to know my son and his mother better while we have this rare free time together. Since we'll be sharing him for the rest of our lives, why not start this minute?

"You felt strongly enough about Ric's Italian ties to come to Genoa in search of them. Let's not waste your efforts this trip. It's a fact you're here with our son. Until you have to go back, we'll enjoy him. I swear I won't do anything you don't want me to."

If there was one thing she knew about Ric, it was that he'd stand by his word.

"We'll fill our days with fun and laughter. It's been ages for me, and I daresay for you since that's happened."

There was a nuance in his voice. A longing for something he wanted, needed to trust. Her heart ached for him. Between that and his promise to be circumspect around her, his logic had once more defeated her.

She kissed the baby's soft cheek to hide her emotions. "I'll need to let my sister know I won't be coming home quite yet."

A glint of satisfaction lit his eyes for a moment. "There's a seaside restaurant further along the coast with the most luscious purple grapes hanging from the ceiling. You won't be able to resist them. The food just keeps coming. Taramasalata, tahini, kebabs, dolmades, eggs, feta cheese and homemade bread and beer. You'll love it. So will our *piccolo*."

Again the years seemed to have fallen off him. Despite her effort not to feel anything, his excitement was contagious, infecting her. He was right about one thing. For the rest of their lives they'd be parenting Ric. A few more days together while they got to know each other better would pave the way for harmony in the future.

Sami had to be honest and admit she wanted this, too. Knowing what made Ric tick would give her more insight into him when their son was older and wanted to talk about him during times of separation.

She'd had hundreds of talks with her grandparents about the mother and father she never knew. Without their input, her life wouldn't have been as rich. For her baby's sake, she would stop worrying about Eliana for the time being and amass as many memories as possible with his father for the time they had left.

CHAPTER SEVEN

Sami had done some snorkeling in Southern California, but nothing as exciting as this trip to the sea caves near Cape Gata. Taking advantage of the warm weather, they'd gone snorkeling to different spots over the last two days. In that time she'd become addicted. With Mara and Daimon along, they could all take turns spelling each other off to swim and watch the baby.

Today, after climbing some cliffs, Sami followed Ric around in the crystal-clear waters while he identified new varieties of fish for her. He'd spent a lot of years in these waters and had obtained his SCUBA certification in his teens. This afternoon had been their coolest day; the temperature had only climbed to sixty-seven degrees. It was warm enough to enjoy being in the boat, but her wetsuit felt good once she'd entered the water with her goggles and fins.

Every time they returned to the cruiser for a snack and a drink, Ric asked her if she'd had enough, but she shook her head and rolled over the side to hunt for new species. He stayed right with her. This round he pointed out mullet and a school of colorful perch. What a delight!

But the next time she lifted her head out of the water, she was surprised to see the sun much lower in the sky. Feeling herself getting tired, she made a signal to Ric that she was ready to get back.

Sami hadn't gone far when an ugly-looking brown fish she hadn't seen before swam directly for her. Before she could think, Ric grabbed her hips and pulled her out of its path. When they reached the ladder on the back of the boat, she pulled off her head gear. "What happened out there?"

Ric removed his gear and tossed both apparatuses in the boat. "You barely escaped the sting from the front fin of a weever fish. Are you all right?"

"I'm fine."

For the last while they'd had such a wonderful time swimming in different waters, she'd forgotten he could look that forbidding. Their bodies brushed against each other from the wake of some other boats passing in the distance.

"I've been stung by one before, so it's obviously not fatal, but its poison is stronger than a wasp sting. They sink in the sand to hide. He came in front of you so fast, I almost didn't get you out of the way in time."

Because of his protective instinct, his dark eyes continued to peruse her features, as if he were still doubting her. By now she was feeling fragile, but it was his nearness that had brought on a need for more oxygen.

"Thank you for saving me," she whispered. With their mouths so close, she ached to her bones to taste him. From sunup to sundown she'd had the time of her life playing with him. There was no one more intelligent or exciting.

But so much togetherness had resulted in her desire for him growing out of control. If she gave in to the temptation to press her lips to his right now, then she was worse than a fool. Calling on the little self-control she had left, she turned back to the ladder.

As she hoisted herself into the boat, she wasn't able to escape the touch of his hands on her hips. He might be trying to help her, but they clung to her as if he were having difficulty letting her go. Weakness attacked her body, making it almost impossible to function.

Thankfully Mara and Daimon were there to greet them and provide towels. Otherwise she would have proven Ric right and thrown herself in his arms because she could no longer resist him.

Without looking at him, she dashed down to the galley to remove her wetsuit. After a shower, she changed into the sweats and T-shirt she'd bought in Paphos the other day. Once dressed, she hurried back up to lavish her emotions on the baby, but Ric was holding him.

As she came forward, he gave his son's dear little head a loving kiss before handing him over. The baby immediately snuggled into her neck. "Our son has missed you," Ric observed. "There's nothing like a mother's love."

"I noticed him clinging to you before I came along. He knows his *papa* now."

Her comment produced a light in his eyes. "I think you're right." On that note he helped them into their life jackets and took his time buckling her up. His gaze rested on her. The look of longing in his eyes sent warmth spiraling through her bloodstream. Her desire for him was so palpable, he couldn't help but notice. Yet he still kept his promise not to do anything she didn't want him to do. *That was the problem.*

The other two stayed in the rear of the boat, leaving Ric to take the wheel. He finally started the engine for the trip back. En route he surprised her by pulling into a marina where there was a wonderful seafood taverna. The place featured dancing and bouzouki music. When he asked her to dance, she declined. No more touching.

Ric didn't seem to mind she'd turned him down. He ate up the attention their little boy drew from waiters and patrons alike. Everyone raved over the beautiful baby. Daimon and Ric took pictures. At the rate he'd been snapping photos on their outings, he'd fill that second scrapbook in no time.

After experiencing another halcyon day, they cruised home through the calm blue water. Except for certain breathless moments she was never prepared for, Sami discovered she was comfortable with Ric. Whether they built sand castles on an isolated beach with their son, or walked along in companionable silence, she relished every second with him.

On the ride home, she stayed up in front of the boat with him to shield the baby from the wind, glad for the obvious excuse because she didn't like to be apart from him. Last night had been the worst. After they'd bathed the baby together and put him down after his bottle, Ric got out some maps and talked about their plans for today before he'd disappeared from her room. She hadn't wanted him to go. She'd almost begged him to stay. That was forbidden.

Sami decided he'd left the villa to conduct the vital business he'd mentioned. It had to be then, or early in the morning. She didn't know and didn't dare ask. One thing she was certain of: he continued to see to the baby around four every morning. Mara told her he was always up before she could take a turn. That brought a secret smile to Sami's lips.

Tonight as they neared the point, she verged on panic because it dawned on her they only had two more days left until he had to return to Genoa. So far Ric had honored his promise to keep things under control by including Mara and Daimon in their activities.

Perversely she hoped he would ask her to stay up with him for a little while tonight after everyone else had gone to bed, if only to talk. Even though she knew it wouldn't be a good idea, the realization that there'd never be nights like this again once she went back to Reno tore her apart.

Within minutes he drove the boat to the dock. Before long they entered the villa. Ric carried the baby while Sami followed him with the carrycot and diaper bag. As they walked down the hall past the living room to the stairs, an unfamiliar female voice called to him.

Out of the corner of her eye, Sami watched a stunning visitor with stylish black hair hurry toward him dressed in elegant eggshell pleated pants and a peacock-blue sweater. She resembled Ric. If it weren't for the baby, Sami was convinced his sister would have thrown her arms around his neck. A stream of Italian escaped her lips. She sounded distressed.

"Claudia?" Ric said in a low voice. "Speak English, *per favore*. If I'd known you were coming, I would have met your plane. Is Marco with you?"

"No."

Ric's eyes glittered with emotion, enough to convince Sami something was wrong. "Meet my house guest Christine Argyle from Reno, Nevada."

The introduction proved to Sami he hadn't told anyone about her. Otherwise he would have added something like "You know—the woman I was entombed with in that avalanche."

"How do you do," Claudia responded. Though polite, she was clearly impatient to talk to him alone.

"Sami? This is my only sister, Claudia Rossi. She and her husband, Marco, live near the family palazzo in Genoa."

"It's very nice to meet you, Claudia. We've just returned from snorkeling and are a mess and exhausted. Since you and your brother will want to talk alone, I'll get the baby's bath started."

"I'd rather you stayed." Ric spoke before she could take the baby from him. He turned to his sister. "What emergency has brought you down here?"

"That's what I came to find out."

Ric's brows formed a black line. "Are Vito and Donata having problems again? I'd hoped they were doing better since he's taken over the operations of the company."

Claudia shook her head. "That's not what this is about. Yesterday Eliana called and asked me to go Christmas shopping with her."

His lips formed a thin line. "So this has to do with my fiancée."

"Yes. We had dinner afterward and I asked her how the wedding plans were coming. She told me you would know the answer better than she did. Then she got up from the table and said she had to go home. She walked off without her packages."

"Eliana should never have involved you."

Claudia's gaze flicked to Sami, then back to him. "I didn't know what to do. I've tried to reach you, but you've turned off your phone. I told Marco this was serious and he agreed I should fly down here and find out what's going on."

Ric wasn't at all surprised Eliana had engineered Claudia's visit. She knew how far to go to create an emergency without giving away her secret.

Eliana had been waiting for him to break the silence and tell her he was giving up his son for her and he'd had the title reinstated. But the wait had gone on too long, so she'd resorted to other tactics. By involving his sister when Eliana had promised to keep quiet until Christmas Eve, she'd made a fatal mistake.

Trust was everything to Ric. Without it a marriage could survive, but for all the wrong reasons.

"Let's sit down, shall we?"

When they were seated around the fireplace he said, "Sami and I have a story to tell you. It's a true story."

As the revelations about the avalanche and Sami's pregnancy unfolded, Claudia's worried expression underwent a drastic transformation. "He's really your baby?" she blurted in complete shock.

It *was* so shocking, no one would ever understand what had happened to two desperate people trying to hold on to life eleven months ago.

"*Si.* Already he's the joy of my life. Why don't you hold him, then you'll know beyond a doubt he has the Degenoli genes."

Ric walked over to his baby-hungry sister and put his son in her arms. He undid the quilt so she could see his limbs, too. The movement brought the baby awake. His eyelids with their black lashes fluttered open.

She looked down at him. "*Oh*—you little angel—"

Her cry of emotion was so heartfelt, he and Sami exchanged glances.

Claudia lifted a wet face. "I see the whole family in him. I see his mother in him, too." She smiled at Sami. "He's the most adorable baby I ever laid eyes on."

The second she spoke, little Ric burst into tears, not liking the strange face and voice. He turned, looking for his father. It caused Ric's heart to leap that his son wanted him. He had never heard him cry like that before, and he picked him back up to hold him. Once in his arms, the baby calmed right down.

"Oh, Ric." Claudia laughed through her tears and stood up so she could get another look at him. Already his sister was smitten with her new nephew. She deserved a baby of her own. If it hadn't been for the avalanche, she might not have lost hers.

But if it hadn't been for the avalanche…

"Eliana won't consider visitation."

"What?" With that one exclamation, he knew which side his sister stood on.

"Eliana asked me to give him up by signing away my parental rights. She's given me until the twenty-fourth to tell her my answer. Otherwise the marriage is off."

Claudia's eyes closed tightly for a minute. "If she said that, then she doesn't know the most important thing about you."

Ric was gratified to hear that. "There's something else, Claudia." He told her he'd had the title abolished. "You've always known I find it an archaic custom that should never have existed in the first place. Once the word is out, I'll have made a lot of enemies, but it doesn't matter."

Her eyelids flew open. "How long ago did you petition the court?"

"After Papa's funeral. Two days ago my attorney called and told me it's official. I'm no longer Count Degenoli. The title's gone forever so no one in our family's future will ever have to be hurt by it."

"Does Eliana know what you've done?" she cried.

"Yes. I told her when she came down here earlier in the week. But I've told Mario I don't want this story leaked to the press until Eliana and I have resolved things. I'm not about to embarrass her or her family."

"Of course not. You wouldn't do that." She suddenly threw her arms around him, baby and all. "I'm so glad,

Ric! When Vito hears this, I honestly believe it could make him a new man. He never felt good enough for Papa, and has always felt inferior to you.

"I think it's the real reason he's always had problems, especially since he got back from military service. He hasn't felt as though he fitted in. This will force him to reevaluate his thinking."

"It would be nice if we could be brothers again in the real sense. That's what I'm hoping for."

She hung on to his arm. "Ever since the avalanche, you've been different. What's happened to you and Sami defies description."

"Discovering I have a son has changed my entire world. I've been committed to Eliana, but without being able to have Ric in our lives, I can't marry her if she won't agree to visitation."

"Of course you can't." His sister eyed the baby. "I've learned to care for her very much and am so sorry for this terrible hurt, but if she thought I would come to her defense on this, then she doesn't know me either. I'd give anything to have a son like baby Ric, even if he weren't mine."

Bless you, Claudia.

"By forcing you to choose between her and your child when it doesn't have to be that way, she'll be making the greatest mistake of her life." Her voice shook. "I need to talk to Eliana in person and convince her of that. Maybe I can get her to put back the date of the wedding for a little while longer until she gets over the worst of the shock and can think clearly."

Ric shook his head. "It won't do any good. It's the title she wants back, but that can't happen now." If anyone could succeed, it would be Claudia. But in his gut, Ric had the premonition neither Eliana or her father would give an inch.

"Thank heaven!" She kissed his cheek. "If you and Sami will excuse me, I've got to phone Marco and tell him I'll be flying back in the morning."

"While you do that, Sami and I are going to get our son ready for bed. Tomorrow we'll all have breakfast and see you off at the airport."

His gaze fell on Sami who said goodnight to his sister, then walked out of the living room with him. After they reached the bedroom at the top of the stairs to start Ric's bath, she glanced at him. "She sounded so emotional when she held the baby. Aren't they able to have children?"

"Yes, but in the aftermath of the avalanche that killed our father, Claudia suffered a miscarriage. She'd been two months along at the time."

"Oh, no— That would have been so devastating for her."

"Our babies would only have been two months apart."

Sami made a soulful sound. "The poor darling. To see you with a baby you had no idea was alive has to be bittersweet for her. She needs to get pregnant again."

"I agree. The doctor says it would be the best thing for her, but Marco says she's been fighting it for fear of losing another one."

"Pat had a miscarriage between children. She went

through the same fear before she got pregnant again. It's a very frightening time."

Ric dripped water on the part of the baby's tummy that wasn't submerged. His little legs kicked so hard, he splashed water. He was a miracle. The idea of a permanent separation from him and the mother who had born him was anathema to Ric.

"I saw that fear with Claudia," he murmured, "but tonight that all seems far away. I'm still celebrating the birth of our son and there's no room for sadness right now." He kissed his cheeks. "You know, I think he's hungry."

"I'm sure he is since it's an hour past his usual time. I'll get a new bottle for him and you can feed him."

"After he's asleep I need to talk to you privately, away from the villa. I'll ask Claudia to listen for him. Between her and Mara, he'll be well taken care of while we take a drive to the harbor. It's one of the major attractions I think is best seen at night."

Sami felt all fluttery inside as Ric drove them along the coast road to the city's harbor.

She'd been waiting to be alone with him. Tonight he looked marvelous in a dark green crew-neck sweater and jeans. The estate car smelled of the soap he'd used in the shower. Combined with his own male scent, her seduction was complete, but he had no idea what his nearness was doing to her. Except that wasn't true. She was sure he did, but he wouldn't act on it.

She forced herself to concentrate on the sights out the

window. Tourists from all over the world—lovers, old couples, teenagers—meandered in and out of the colorful shops beautifully decorated for Christmas. The holiday excitement was contagious. Cooking aromas drifted from the restaurants lining the curving seawall. The area was made all the more romantic by the sight of Paphos Castle lit up for Christmas against a dark blue sky.

Ric pulled to a stop on a rise away from the other cars so she could get a good view. "This used to be a Byzantine fort that was rebuilt by the Lusignians, then redone by the Venetians and finally restored by the Ottomans. What you're looking at is one of two towers built in 1222. Sadly, the other was destroyed by an earthquake."

"Being on Cyprus is like living in an ancient open-air archaeological museum. I'm in awe. Thank you for bringing me here, Ric." She clasped her hands in her lap. "I'd be remiss if I didn't thank you for everything you've done for me the last few days, the excursions in the boat—I appreciate how much you've gone out of your way to make this an enchanting time."

"I've enjoyed it, too. More than you know. It's given me time to think about the future. That's what I want to talk to you about. Our lives are going to be connected from here on out. We might as well start laying the groundwork."

Suddenly her pulse sped up. She swung her blond head toward him. "How can you plan anything when you don't know if you're getting married or not?"

"The one doesn't have anything to do with the other.

No matter what happens between Eliana and me, Ric is a part of my life now. I want to talk about how you and I can share our son with the least amount of difficulty."

"There's no such animal, Ric, not when we live on separate continents."

"Then maybe we can change that."

Her heart pounded outrageously. "How?"

He stared at her over his strong arm stretched across the top of the steering wheel. "If you moved to Cyprus."

Sami's eyelids squeezed shut. "You can't be serious."

"Just hear me out. You and Ric would live at the villa. There's a department of computer engineering at the university in Limassol. It's a ten-minute helicopter ride from my house to the campus. With Mara and Daimon here to help, you could get your master's degree and be with our son the same as you would in Reno."

"I don't know Greek!"

"With your brain, you'll pick it up fast and I'll help you."

"Ric—you don't really mean what you're saying."

"Why not? If I'm married, I'll fly down from Genoa every Friday evening after work and fly back Monday morning. You'd have that time to get away, study, travel. Anything. It's a workable solution to our problem so our son sees both of us on a regular basis. We'd bring your sister and family over to visit often. Neither Claudia nor Vito's wife, Donata, would be able to stay away. Donata wants a baby. When Vito sees himself in Ric, he'll want one, too."

"And of course Eliana would be all right with that—"

She was so shaken, her voice was virtually unrecognizable.

"If we're married, then she could either come with me or stay in Genoa. The choice is hers."

"She'd never stand for it."

"Eliana would have to. It would be part of our marriage agreement."

"The idea is ludicrous."

Something flickered in the dark recesses of his eyes. "Can you think of a better one?"

Her thoughts were reeling. "I couldn't just move here—"

"Not even for Ric's sake? How much are you willing to sacrifice to give him a stable home with his own mother and father?"

"That's not fair."

He moved his arm and rested it on the back of the seat. His fingers were within inches of her hair. "I can make it fairer by providing for you and Ric so you don't have to worry about money and paying back student loans."

"You're not my husband!"

"I'm Ric's father," he shot back calmly. "My son means everything to me."

She trembled. "He's my raison d'être!"

"Precisely. That's why we need each other to make this work so everyone's happy. I want to give you and Ric everything. You went through the whole pregnancy alone and have been raising him without help. Now that you've found I'm alive, I'm prepared to do whatever it takes. It's my turn and my right as Ric's father."

"I'm overwhelmed by your generosity, but what you're asking is impossible."

"Not impossible—practical. Flying down here once a week to see Ric makes more sense than for me to fly to Reno on a weekly basis to see him. But I'll arrange it if I have to."

"You couldn't do that—" she exclaimed, alarmed for him. "Your life wouldn't be worth living. You wouldn't have a company to go back to, and your wife wouldn't be able to handle it!"

"Nevertheless it's what I'll do if you can't see yourself moving here. I'll give Vito more responsibility. Claudia's observations about him have given me food for thought."

"But Ric—"

"No buts, Sami. After being trapped together and given a second chance at life, how can we not give our son as much joy as possible? If you can't bring yourself to move, I'll buy a home on Lake Tahoe to be near you. The high elevation makes a perfect setting."

"When were you there?"

"Right before I started college, I traveled to the States with some friends. It's one of the most beautiful lakes I've ever seen. I'll buy a boat for Ric and me to enjoy. But as I said, you have a ready-made home right here on the Mediterranean. Ric will grow up being trilingual, which will be a great advantage to him."

As usual, he had a way of getting to her. She couldn't argue with his logic. He had the financial means to make anything he wanted happen, but he refused to consider the elephant in the room. "Until you know what Eliana has decided, then there's no more point to this discussion."

"I agree. I've told you what I intend to do one way or the other. You have until Christmas Eve to decide what plan sounds best to you," he said on a satisfied note.

He started the car and they headed back to the villa. In the process, he had to remove his arm which brushed her shoulder. The slightest touch sent little fingers of delight through her body. She grasped at any topic to cover her reaction. "Maybe Claudia will be able to make Eliana see reason."

In the darkness of the interior, his expression looked almost savage, sending a different shiver down her spine. "If by that time my fiancée hasn't come to terms with everything on her own, then she's not the person I thought she was."

He sounded so distant, she couldn't pick up on anything else.

"Maybe she doesn't have the capacity to love without qualification. Some people don't. But if growing up as a princess with money and power means so much to her that she can't accept your situation, then that's something else."

Sami had to give Matt credit. Even though the news about her pregnancy had been brutally painful for him, he'd still insisted he wanted to marry her and would love the baby. But that was before she'd discovered Ric was alive and wanted his son.

If she decided to marry Matt now and live in Oakland with him, Ric would buy himself a home there in order to be with the baby. There was no way out. By coming to Genoa, she'd changed destiny.

"In a few days I'll have my answer, Sami."

She bowed her head. "I'm beginning to understand why you did away with your title. More than ever I'm thankful you abolished it. I want our son to grow up having a normal life, never thinking he's better than anyone else."

He exhaled a heavy sigh. "That's the whole idea."

If Eliana didn't love Ric enough to let go of her pride and accept his child, then she didn't deserve him. Having said that to herself, Sami had to admit she'd fallen in love with him. Crazily in love so she could scarcely breathe whenever she heard his voice or saw him enter a room.

"Ric? Tell me something honestly."

"I'll do my best," he said in a slight drawl.

"Was there another woman in your past before Eliana? Someone you wanted to marry?"

His bark of laughter wounded her. "You think my heart's desire spurned me years ago, putting me off women for the rest of my life?"

Her cheeks grew warm. She shouldn't have said anything.

"Don't try to figure me out. You won't succeed. The truth is, I thought I was in love with every woman I got close to. But to my parents' regret, I could never see myself married to any of them." He shifted in the seat. "What about you? Why weren't you married long before now?"

His question brought her up short. "I never met the right one."

"The right one… I wonder if there is such a thing."

"Did your father press you to marry Eliana?"

"He had his hopes, but no." His answer was unequivocal. "I decided to marry her of my own free will, for my own reasons and no one else's."

She hadn't been expecting that revelation. It hit her with the force of the avalanche. His comment put a different slant on everything. After finally deciding to spend the rest of his life with Eliana, she had disappointed him by wanting the title and not being willing to accept his baby. The hurt had gone straight to his heart and meant he was suffering, but he'd never let it show. Sami wished she could shield him from that pain.

"Did your parents have a good marriage?" she asked quietly.

"For an arranged one, it worked remarkably well. Father had his affairs and Mother overlooked them."

That would explain his cynicism.

"I don't know about my siblings' marriages at this stage," he went on speaking. "They were both in love, but these are early days with more difficult times to come. What else would you like to know?" They'd arrived at the villa. He parked the car in the drive and shut off the engine.

"I'm sorry if I've offended you with my questions."

"Offended—" He turned to her. The moonlight pouring through the windshield reflected in his black eyes. "I find it totally refreshing. Nothing's changed since we were caught in the avalanche. I found *you* totally refreshing then, too. For the first time in my life, I was with a woman who knew nothing about me, who couldn't have identified me.

"We took each other as we found each other, Sami. No preconceptions. Whatever came out of you was genuine and honest. I believe that foundation put into motion what happened between us. After spending time with you, it's not a mystery to me any longer."

It wasn't for her either. But she feared that if she stayed in the car another minute, she'd blurt out her love for him. "We'd better go in and check on Ric, just in case he awakened and found us both gone."

"Don't leave yet," he suggested. "Mara would have called me if there was a problem. I thought with this full moon we'd take a walk on the beach. The light brings the dollar fish to the surface. You'd enjoy the sight. I brought a jacket for you."

Heaven help her but she didn't want to go in yet. At least walking would keep her body in motion. Sitting out here in the dark with him amounted to an open invitation to forget rules and beg him to kiss her. But if he did what she wanted, it would be her fault. She wished he *weren't* so honorable, but of course she didn't really mean it.

"As long we're only gone a short while."

"We'll come back whenever you say."

If there were no Eliana, he'd have a long wait.

He reached in back for the black leather bomber jacket and handed it to her. After thanking him, she got out of the car and put it on before he could come around. It was too big, the sleeves too long, but it smelled of him and she loved the feeling of being wrapped in it.

They made their way past the marina, their bodies close together, but not touching. No one else was out walking along the shore. The moonlight made a pale gold path across the water, following their progress. Lights from a cruiser far out from the coast twinkled in the darkness. Sometimes perfection was too perfect. This was one of those times, deepening her ache for Ric.

Keep moving.

"Come look over here, Sami."

She'd been so deep in her thoughts about him, she hadn't realized he'd stopped. When she turned, she saw he was hunkered down close to the water. She walked over.

"Oh—they look exactly like silver dollars!"

"These fish like to come up to the surface at night and moon-bathe."

"How adorable. They look like they don't have a worry in the world. I'd like to do that myself. Where are their babies?"

He chuckled. "I've never thought about it. In summer we'll swim here at night and find out."

He was sounding as though her move to Cyprus was already a fait accompli. "They don't sting?"

"No. Like our son, they're harmless, but not helpless. If they sense danger, they disappear like those heavenly bodies you once compared us to. Amazing how our separate orbits collided again." He stared up at her. "Only this time I can see your hair. Its glow rivals the moonlight. I'm surprised it didn't illuminate our heavenly prison. Once we'd reconciled ourselves to our fate, that time with you *was* heavenly, Sami. Wondrous."

Tears stung her eyelids. "I'll never forget it. Every time I look at Ric, I remember."

"That's why he's perfect, because it was so perfect for us. You thrilled me, Sami."

She was dying inside. "Please don't say things like that and make this harder than it already is," she begged him. "Let's go back and promise not to talk about it again."

He rose to his full height. Ric possessed a virility she had no immunity against. "I promised not to do anything you didn't want me to, but you can't make me promise *that*. You became a part of me. We became parts of each other and it produced our baby. From now on we'll be wrestling with that reality. It's pointless to pretend otherwise."

Sami bit her lip. "So you think talking about it is going to help?"

A grimace marred his hardened features. "No."

Not waiting for anything else he might have said, she started running and didn't stop until she entered the villa. No one was around as she dashed up the stairs to her bedroom and walked over to the crib. Their baby slept soundly. While she looked down at him, examining every precious part, Sami felt Ric's hands slide to her shoulders from behind. She hadn't heard him enter the room. The contact made her feel light-headed.

"I've made a decision." When he spoke, his lips brushed her temple. "We're going to fly back to Genoa with Claudia in the morning. I need to talk to Eliana in person. She should have made up her mind by now. The fact that she hasn't phoned yet seems to prove she doesn't want the marriage. I refuse to play games and wait until the twenty-fourth. Be ready by six to drive to the airport."

CHAPTER EIGHT

AFTER squeezing her shoulders gently, Ric let her go and vanished from the room. Sami stood there for a long time afterward before she started packing. Even when she'd finally put on her cotton pajamas and climbed under the covers to go to bed, she could still feel the imprint of his hands. Talking about the past reminded her how much pleasure he'd given her. If she was going to be haunted by those memories for the rest of her life, she'd go mad.

Sami didn't know when she fell asleep, but it was only ten to three when the baby's crying brought her wide-awake. She turned on the lamp and flew out of bed to pick him up. Since coming to Cyprus, this was the first time she'd gotten up with him in the night. Ric had claimed that job from the beginning.

Though she tried to settle him down, he cried harder. Afraid he was sick, she put him on her bed to change him, but saw nothing wrong. She felt his face and forehead, but he wasn't running a temperature. While she put a clean diaper on him, a disheveled Ric, wearing a brown robe, swept into the room barefooted.

"What do you think's wrong?" He sounded anxious. "Our *piccolo* has never awakened this early in the night."

"He probably had a gas pain."

The second the baby looked at his father, he cried harder than ever. On a burst of inspiration, Sami snapped up his stretchy suit and handed him to Ric. The moment he cuddled him against his shoulder and spoke Italian to him in an incredibly tender tone, the baby quieted down. Every so often a little half sob escaped, shaking his body.

She smiled. "It's obvious there's nothing wrong that his *papa* can't fix."

"Sami..."

"It's true. He's feels safe with you. Every son wants a father like you, but not all sons are that lucky." She walked over to the dresser for another bottle of formula. "Here. While you feed him, I'll go to sleep for what's left of the night."

She turned off the light and went back to bed, assuming he'd sit in the chair as he always did. Instead, he walked around the other side of the bed and lay down on top of the covers, putting the baby between them. "I think he'll be happier if he's here with both of us."

No, Ric—

"He's hungry!"

Sami could tell. The baby made noises while he was wolfing down his formula, provoking laughter from Ric that shook the bed. "After watching you eat, I've decided he must take after you."

"So you've noticed."

Heat spread through her body. She noticed every single detail about him. "It was hard not to when you ordered a third helping of those *mezes* at the seaside restaurant."

"I confess I'm a fish lover."

"They were delicious."

"If Ric grows up here, he'll become addicted. Do you have anything like them in Reno?"

"Not even remotely and you know it! It'll be hamburgers and pizza." The idea of living on Cyprus hadn't left her mind, but she could never do it. It wouldn't be fair to Eliana or their marriage.

And if he didn't marry her?

It still wouldn't be right. In everyone's eyes Sami would be a kept woman. But in Reno, she'd be the head of her own home. He'd be a father who came on visitation, like other divorced fathers. They wouldn't be sleeping together. She'd made her mind up about that, too. Sami hadn't lived her life this long to end up being a man's lover and nothing else, even if that man was the most wonderful man on earth.

She had no illusions where he was concerned. He'd told her he thought he'd loved every woman with whom he'd ever had an intimate relationship, but he'd never wanted to marry any of them. Whatever reason had caused him to propose to Eliana had its underpinnings based on other things he hadn't chosen to reveal.

Sami believed Eliana would break down and agree to anything to be married to Ric. She just needed more convincing, and was waiting for Ric to come to her. Well, her plan had succeeded because he was cutting this vacation short to be with her again. Six o'clock would be here before they knew it.

A loud burp resonated in the room. She grinned. "I heard that. Why don't you put him back down in the crib so you can get some sleep before we leave?"

"Did you hear that, *figlio mio?* Your *mamma* wants to get rid of us."

"I do," she lied.

She felt the side of the bed dip. "Then we'll let you get your beauty sleep. In case you were wondering, you don't need it."

Keep that up and I'm yours forever.

At nine the next morning, Ric's jet landed in Genoa. During the flight Sami had got better acquainted with Claudia, who was a lovely person in her own right. They talked about her miscarriage and Ric's birth. Sami felt that in other circumstances they could be close friends.

A limousine was waiting at the airport to transport them. As Sami glanced around before getting in, she noticed the hood. The special ornament was missing!

Like Pharoah, who'd had the name of Moses erased from every pillar and historical record, Ric had wiped his life clean of its former title. His bodyguards no longer called him Excellency. If all of this pleased him, he didn't mention it. Naturally his thoughts were on the meeting he was about to have with Eliana which accounted for his deep preoccupation.

"We'll take you home first, Claudia."

They passed many of the city's architectural wonders

and eventually reached Claudia's stately villa, one of the Degenoli properties. Sami could tell it was by the gold crest of the ancient seaman on the grillwork of the gate.

Claudia embraced her brother with the promise to get together later. Then she gave Sami a hug. "I can't wait for Marco to meet you and the baby."

Sami grasped her hand. "I'll call you," she whispered out of Ric's hearing. His sister pressed Sami's fingers, as if to say message received. She was a quick study and understood it wasn't an idle remark. After another kiss to little Ric's cheeks, Claudia got out of the limo and ran inside the villa.

Ric told the driver to head to the palazzo. He must have asked him to take the scenic route. They drove slowly through an area Ric pointed out the market of Saint Porphyrius. Local craftsmen displayed their Christmas products along the streets, and squares of the old town were dotted with huge nativity scenes.

Sami loved him desperately for always putting her pleasure and comfort first. She was no longer the same person who'd arrived in Italy fearing a bad reaction from Ric's father, even if she were able to find him. Since discovering Ric was alive, *she'd* come alive. Ric had become her life.

The limousine rounded a corner and climbed toward a beautiful medium-sized palace on the hill. "How beautiful!" she exclaimed to him. "What's its history?"

"Genovans call it the Palazzo Vermiglio. It was built in the seventeenth century. In English it means *vermillion,* so named because of its orangish-red exterior."

"I noticed the unique color right off. The interior must be incredible, too."

"Would you like to see it?"

"Not today, Ric. Remembering your reason for returning to Genoa, don't you know the last thing on my mind is sightseeing?"

"I'll make this the one exception." His playful tone threw her. He could be a tease. She'd seen evidence of it before, but this time she wasn't amused.

"Ric—I'm serious."

"So am I."

The limousine passed through a gate and wound around to the side. When it stopped, several of Ric's bodyguards opened the doors. He got out to help her with the baby.

"We'll go to your room first," he said in an aside before he spoke Italian with the others.

Your room?

Sami moaned. She had to be all kinds of a fool not to have realized this was his home. But the grandeur of it astounded her. How many men born in such circumstances would consider doing away with their title? Seeing where he lived gave her new insight into Eliana's pain.

She looked down at the baby asleep in his carrycot. When she'd told Ric their little boy reminded him of a prince in a fairy tale, she hadn't realized she was only speaking the truth.

"If you've caught up with your thoughts, we'll go in." His low voice curled beneath her skin to resonate through her nervous system.

The men took their things so he could cup her elbow. Bemused, she walked through the doors of the side entrance with him. He introduced her to an older-looking staff member named Mario who spoke in rapid Italian to Ric calling him Excellency. Uh-oh.

Ric guided her to an ornate staircase, not giving her a chance to ask questions. They started up the white marble steps to the next floor lined with paintings and tapestries. Halfway down the hall Mario opened the double doors to a sumptuous suite.

"This is your room, Sami," Ric explained, "and next door is the nursery."

She was so staggered by the opulence, she forgot to walk, and then had to hurry to catch up with him as he strode to another set of open doors. A female staff member he introduced as Sofia was waiting for them.

A cry escaped her throat when she saw the lavish nursery. Her eyes went to the exquisite crib that must have been in their family for years. "This just couldn't be real!"

One of the only grins she'd seen come from him unexpectedly appeared, making her heart leap. "I assure you it's as real as we are. It was made for the firstborn son of the fifth Count Degenoli. Shall we see how our son likes his new room?"

Before she could respond, a disturbance on the other side of the door had her turning around to see a man who was questioning Sofia in Italian. Sami might not understand the language, but she knew an interrogation when she heard one.

"Vito?" Ric called out. "Speak English, *per favore,* and come in."

Another drop-dead-handsome Italian with black hair entered the room. He was the same height as Ric with certain Degenoli traits that were unmistakable. Sami winced when she noticed a scar on the side of his neck. It came up a little above his jawline, no doubt a burn injury from his military experience.

"Vito? I'd like you to meet Sami, born Christine Argyle from Reno, Nevada. Sami, as you know, Vito's my only brother. He and Donata live in the other wing of the palace."

His brother nodded to her, scrutinizing her from head to toe.

"Sami's the mother of my son, Ric, who so far hasn't awakened since we got off the plane."

She could tell the other man was in shock. He stared at the baby, then at Ric. "So it's true what Claudia told me on the phone last night?"

"Every last word." Ric kissed his son's little cheeks again, then picked him up from the cot and put him on his shoulder. "Come take a good look at him and there'll be no doubt."

Vito walked over to inspect the baby. Pretty soon a smile lit up his dark brown eyes. "With that shape of his hairline, he's yours all right. Donata will have a heart attack when she sees him. She's not feeling well this morning, but she'll be up later."

"Would you like to hold him?" Sami asked.

"It's permitted?" He could be a tease like Ric.

"With my blessing. You and Claudia's husband are his only Italian uncles. His American uncle is married to my only sibling, Pat."

He stared at her a moment longer, digesting her words. Then he took the baby and put him against his shoulder the way Ric had done. "What's his name?"

"Ric Argyle Degenoli."

Vito shook his head. "Who would have thought? Monsignor Tibaldi would say when God took one away in the avalanche, he provided another."

"I believe he *would* say that." Ric responded to the dark humor before his gaze slid to Sami's. "I have to say *we* were the most surprised parents on the planet."

His brother's features sobered. "There's only one person more surprised."

"You're talking about Eliana, of course."

"Who else but your fiancée?"

"I'm going over there at noon to talk to her."

His brother handed the baby back to Sami before he looked at Ric. "Answer me one more question. Is it true you got rid of the title?"

"Yes. We're all on the same playing field now. No more firstborns. After centuries, the Degenoli line is free of its nemesis." Sami heard the fierceness in his voice.

Vito must have heard it, too. He looked stunned. "When did you start proceedings?"

"Soon after Father's funeral, but I had to go through a lot of red tape to make it official."

A nerve throbbed at Vito's temple. "Does Eliana know about it?"

"Yes."

He whistled. "*Mamma* always said you played with fire."

Sami's eyes went to the scar at the side of Vito's neck. Both men had them, though Ric's had been hidden.

"She played with it herself by marrying Papa, wouldn't you agree?"

Silence filled the nursery while the two men communicated in silence. Whatever was going on between them was private. Sami and Pat had shared similar moments throughout their lives. Neither of them had to say a word to get what the other was thinking.

There was still a whole part of Ric she knew nothing about. Though it was none of her business, she wanted to know all his secrets and felt deprived.

Vito broke the silence. "I'll be seeing you later, Signorina Argyle." He touched the baby's cheek with the back of his hand before leaving the room. She went over to the crib and laid Ric down. His lids had closed again. "He looks so cute in there. I do believe he's even made your brother baby-hungry."

"For several reasons, the Degenoli family will never be the same again."

Sami heaved a sigh, dreading what was coming. "Are you going to leave now?"

"Not until you're properly settled."

"Consider it done."

"I've never known a woman so easy to please. In case you do need anything later, just use the house phone and press zero. One of the staff will help you."

"Thank you. Now please stop worrying about me. You go on and meet with your fiancée. I have a feeling it will mean everything that you decided to surprise her," Sami's voice shook.

"Not until you and I have another talk first."

She frowned. "Another talk?"

"I saw your face before Vito left. It's time you knew certain facts about my life I hadn't chosen to reveal yet, but the event facing me today has dictated the moment." She had a sudden foreboding she wasn't going to like it. "Let's go in your room so we won't disturb the baby. What I have to tell you will take a while."

Alarmed by his words, she walked out of the nursery first. Ric followed, but he left the door ajar so they could hear the baby if he cried. Whatever he had to say had made her nervous and she sought refuge in the first available upholstered chair.

He remained standing while he leveled his gaze on her. "Eliana's father is from Milan and one of the wealthiest industrialists in our country. He married a Genovan princess, which makes Eliana one, too. For years I've known of her and many other eligible prospects my parents had in mind for me one day. When I turned twenty-one I told them I wasn't the marrying type so they could stop hoping for something that wasn't going to happen.

"They despaired of me, but didn't take me seriously.

Before my mother died, she begged me to stop being foolish and marry Eliana Fortulezza who would make me a wonderful wife and a beautiful one. It surprised me she had a preference. Because she was so ill, I told her I'd think seriously about it in order to bring her peace of mind. But I had no intention of following through. After Mother's funeral, I put it out of my mind.

"Less than half a year after her death, Father and I traveled to Imst for the wedding of my cousin to an Austrian of nobility. I didn't want to go because I knew Father would harp on me about my bachelor status, but he'd had a bad case of the flu and needed help, so I accompanied him. We stayed at the hotel that brought you and me together. The wedding was held in the Maria Himmelfahrt Church."

"I remember seeing it as I was coming in on the train. You couldn't miss it."

He nodded. "Before we went back to Innsbruck for the flight home, Papa wanted to relax in town for a few more days to get back his strength. On the night before the avalanche hit, he broke down and told me he was in financial trouble. That didn't surprise me. Years earlier Vito and I had learned through our uncle in Paphos that our father was an inveterate gambler."

Sami moaned. "That must have come as a terrible shock."

"At the time, you could have no idea. Considering how much money our father had the ability to lay his hands on, it raised terror in our hearts. The family wealth earned over hundreds of years could be like a gift that kept on giving. But squandered long enough if no one stopped him, one day it would come to an end and be the downfall of the family.

"Vito and I confronted him. He laughed and told us to mind our own business. He told me I had no right to question him because I didn't hold the title yet. In the same breath he told Vito he would never have the right to question what he did because he wasn't the firstborn. I'm convinced that rebuke was the reason my brother signed up for the military.

"He was fed up with Father. Already disillusioned by Father's womanizing, Vito didn't want any part of watching our father gamble away his legacy. Unfortunately Donata thought he'd lost interest in her. Vito was so ashamed of our revered father, who had to be the laughingstock of Genoa, he couldn't talk to her about it. The silence on his end did serious damage to their marriage, yet Donata has held on. Vito's luckier than he knows."

"I'm so sorry, Ric."

He threw his head back. "This gets worse. When I asked Father just how deep his problems were, he told me Eliana's father had covered some big debts for him. The mere mention of her father hit me like a bomb blast because it meant he'd needed help from someone like her father who had the kind of money necessary.

"Father had been living in denial for years and now his problems were horrific. He didn't need to spell it out.

The implication was painfully clear. If I married Eliana, those debts would be forgotten."

Sami shot to her feet. "But that's monstrous!"

"Perhaps now you understand my aversion to the title and all it represented. Evidently my mother had known about my father's gambling problem. It suddenly made sense why on her deathbed she'd pushed me in Eliana's direction as hard as she could. She was always loyal to my father, so she wouldn't have come right out to tell me the truth."

"Oh, Ric…"

"I was sickened by his confession, disgusted. Wounded. And still he wouldn't discuss amounts of money with me. He was too cowardly. For him to force me to marry Eliana meant the stakes were astronomical. Nothing less than her father obtaining the title and possession of the existing Degenoli family assets through his daughter Eliana would satisfy the debt.

"Father must have seen the distaste in my eyes because he actually broke down and cried like a baby. I'd never seen him do that before and I realized he was a broken man cursed by two vices that got a stranglehold on him early in life. When he begged me to marry Eliana to save him, I had to get out of the room."

Sami put a hand to her mouth, too horrified to speak.

"As I opened the door to go downstairs, he screamed at me to make that promise to him. He was on his hands and knees and looked so frail he could have been a hundred years old. I finally told him that in time there would be a marriage in the future, but I would do it for the family's sake, not his. That was the last time I ever saw him alive."

What he'd told her was too awful. She loved him so much and felt so helpless in the face of what she knew. "Does Eliana know all this?"

"No. Her father never worries about stooping to criminal behavior to get his own way. He rules her life in what I consider a criminal way and has shielded her because he's been so sure of the final outcome. For a truly greedy man, money isn't enough. He wanted the title to legitimize him once and for all. I'm the target he's been after all this time, which is why he enabled Father to get in deeper and deeper till he had him completely sewn up with no squirming room."

Sami couldn't stop her shivering. "What will he do when he finds out the title's gone?"

"I have a good idea. Rest assured I'm ready for him."

Ric's life was in danger. Sami could feel it.

"But what about Eliana?" she cried.

He sucked in his breath. "Sadly she's a victim of the same system as her father, whose god is money. She's ruled by him. Since June I've done my best to be good to her in order to save my own sanity and make our forthcoming marriage work. But my father's unexpected death put certain dynamics into motion that forced me to act sooner on my promise to him. In the process I hadn't counted on seeing you again in this life."

Another tremor passed through her body. If anything happened to Ric...

"Our emotional connection created a complication that's had a ripple effect. Instead of immediately getting to know Eliana with the goal of marrying her, I spent time looking for you first. Even though Father had died, I knew at one point I had to honor my commitment. But there's another truth to all this. If it weren't for the promise I made to him, I'd still be looking for you."

Ric...

When Sami had been defending him in the hotel room before learning his identity, she'd said he was the most honorable man she'd ever known. She'd believed it at the time and believed it now to the depth of her soul.

"After you and I were buried under the snow, I was positive my father was already dead. While we waited for the end to come, I realized that promise would never be fulfilled. I prayed for Claudia and Vito who'd be at the mercy of Eliana's father once the funeral services were over. He would swoop in and take everything out from under them. It would read like a novel and make headlines felt throughout the country."

She trembled. "But you *did* live through that avalanche." Since then he'd been carrying this nightmare on his shoulders and standing on the edge of a financial precipice.

History had taught her that kingdoms had been lost or won on the promises sealed with lands and dowries. In this case his father's scandalous behavior had cost their family the Degenoli empire. It wasn't fair. It was an archaic, evil system, just as he'd said.

Her thoughts flew back to the day she'd asked him if he were rich. He'd responded with what she now knew was a riddle. The second Eliana called off the wedding, Ric's family would be ruined. Sami couldn't stand it. If she hadn't come to Italy, none of this would be happening. Ric was in real danger now.

He'd told her he had his own reasons for asking Eliana to marry him. Now that Sami understood what they were, she needed to leave the country. If Eliana's father were pushed too far, he might come after the one thing Ric valued above all else. *Their baby...*

At this point there was only one thing to do, but she needed to get rid of Ric first. "After what you've told me, I can't bear for you to be here any longer. Please don't let me keep you. You need to go to her father and work this out."

He gave an elegant shrug of his shoulders. "There might be nothing to work out now he knows there's no title involved in the transaction. We'll see."

"Ric—there has to be some way to make this right."

"That could be asking too much, Sami. You've heard of the sins of the father, and I'm my father's son with a baby and no title."

There might even be bloodshed. Was that why Ric never took a step without his bodyguards?

Tears coursed down her cheeks. "I'd give anything to help you. What are you going to do?"

He looked so grim, she thought he must be ill. "Whatever I have to." His pain-filled eyes devastated her. "What will you do while I'm gone?"

No matter his pain, he was still worried about her.

Put on a face, Sami. Don't let him know.

"None of us got much sleep last night. I'm going to catch up on mine while the baby has a long nap. Later on I plan to phone my sister and let her know I'm installed in a real palace with the man who refused to be king."

Ric's sharp intake of breath reverberated against the walls. "I don't know when I'll be back. It'll probably be late."

"Take care," she called after him.

CHAPTER NINE

THE second he strode from her room, Sami moved over to the table and pulled out her cell phone to call her sister. Pat wouldn't appreciate being awakened at two in the morning, but this was an emergency. After three rings she picked up.

"Sami?"

"I'm sorry to do this to you, Pat, but I need a favor and don't have time to talk. It's 11:00 a.m. my time. Will you book me on a flight out of Genoa anytime this afternoon or evening my time, leaving for the States? Phone me back when you've got the reservation booked. Love you."

After hanging up, she moved over to the table to use the house phone. When a male staff member answered she said, "Could you connect me with Claudia Rossi, please."

"One moment."

In another thirty seconds Ric's sister came on the line. "Sami?"

"Hello, Claudia. I'm so glad you answered. I'd like to talk to you in person. Do you think we could get together for lunch today? Maybe we could meet at a favorite restaurant of yours?"

"Of course. I'll come by for you at the side entrance. Shall we say in a half hour?" Claudia knew something was wrong and was playing right along. Sami could hug her for it.

"That would be perfect. Thank you."

She put the phone back on the hook.

Since she was already dressed in her suit and white blouse, all she had to do was pack the diaper bag with some formula and diapers she'd need for the flight. She couldn't take her luggage. That would be a dead giveaway. She needed to look like a mother going out for an afternoon with a friend.

When it was time, she put Ric in his carrycot. Just as she was about to walk out, her phone rang. She picked up. "Pat?"

"It's done. Five o'clock on TransItalia to New York. You'll connect with a Continental flight to Reno."

"Bless you. Now I've got to go."

She left the suite and walked down the magnificent hallway with the baby. Several staff people nodded to her. Claudia's limousine was waiting at the side entrance as planned. Little Ric was still asleep.

As Sami climbed inside she whispered, "Can your driver hear us?"

"Not unless I turn on the switch."

"That's good, because I need your help. We need to devise a plan to get me to the airport without Ric's bodyguards catching on."

"You're *leaving?*"

"I have to. Do you know about your father's gambling debts?"

"A little."

"Then I need to tell you everything so you'll understand." On the drive to the villa, Sami poured it all out. It was time Ric's family knew the terrible burdens he'd been carrying and the danger he could be in. "After hearing what a ruthless man Eliana's father is, I wouldn't put it past him to target our baby as a way to make Ric conform."

"I wouldn't either," Claudia said with conviction. "You're doing the right thing and I'm going to help you. Even if Ric never speaks to me again, it will be worth it when he finds out why you left."

Sami squeezed Claudia's hand. "Ric can't stand for me to take the baby away. After the avalanche, he has this fear he might never see him again. But the situation is too volatile for me to stay in Italy any longer."

"Do you know Vito phoned me before you did? Knowing about the rescinding of the title, he's put two and two together and wants you away from the palace. We both agree you need to be gone until this thing with Eliana is resolved one way or another."

Sami heaved a relieved sigh. "Do you have any ideas how to accomplish this? My flight leaves at five o'clock."

"I've eluded my bodyguards from time to time. Leave this to me." For a moment she sounded like her brother in one of his teasing moods.

Claudia pressed the switch and said something in

Italian to the driver. Then she turned it off. "I told him to take us back to the villa where we'll have lunch and stay until five o'clock when you're due back at the palace. He'll pass that information on.

"When we get to the villa, we'll go inside and have lunch. Then we'll hide you in the back of my secretary's car. Signora Bertelli comes every weekday morning at eight and leaves by three. Her car is parked in the rear near my study. The guards won't have any idea. You can give her your instructions on the way to the airport."

Though Sami was in deep pain, she smiled at Claudia. "You're brilliant."

Ric left the Fortulezza estate for the last time. His business was finished and his agony over. Every asset including money and properties of the Degenoli fortune were now in the hands of Eliana's father.

Thanks to Ric's father, neither he nor Vito had a job, and neither he nor his siblings had a roof over their heads.

At least not in Genoa.

But he'd managed to salvage his mother's assets, enough for all of them to start a new life on Cyprus and be a real family.

He was free. Free in every sense of the word.

His heart pounded like steel striking an anvil. All he could think of was Sami and his son. He climbed in the limousine and told the driver to take him back to the palazzo. Once they arrived at the side entrance, he raced inside and took the steps two at a time to reach the second floor.

"Sami?" He knocked on her suite door. When she didn't answer, he opened it and called her name again. No answer. Her things were still around. He hurried through to the nursery. Ric wasn't in there. Maybe she'd put him in the stroller and had taken him for a walk.

He phoned Mario. "Have you seen our guests?"

"No. She and the baby left with your sister for lunch at her villa around eleven-thirty. As far as I know, they're still there."

"Thank you."

He hung up and called Claudia. All he got was her voice messaging. Frustrated, he phoned Carlo. "I understand Signorina Argyle and my son are still with my sister."

"That's right. Your sister told the driver the signorina would be leaving at five to return to the palazzo." Ric glanced at his watch. It was four-thirty. "She's not answering her phone. Do me a favor and go to the door. I need to speak to her. Tell her to call me."

"Bene."

A minute later his phone rang. "Claudia? I understand Sami's still there. Will you put her on?"

"I'm afraid she's no longer here."

"Then where is she? I'm at the palazzo and there's no sign of her or Ric."

"Listen, Ric—"

He heard her hesitation. A band tightened around his lungs. Whenever Claudia started out a sentence like that, she was afraid of something. "Where is she?"

"A-at the airport," she stammered.

He knew it. "When does her plane leave?"

"Five."

"What airline?"

"TransItalia to New York. Don't be angry. She was afraid Eliana's father might come after your baby and—"

"I know exactly how Sami's mind works." He cut her off. "But I know something she doesn't and everything's going to be fine, so don't worry. I'll tell you all the details later."

He hung up and phoned Carlo. "Get out to the airport and stop the TransItalia flight that's supposed to leave at five for New York. Signorina Argyle and my son are on it."

"But how could they be?" he asked in bewilderment.

"You're dealing with my sister, who knows every trick in the book. I'm taking the helicopter and will meet you there."

On his way to the pad at the rear of the palace he phoned Mario. "Instruct the staff to gather up everything Signorina Argyle left in the suite and have it delivered to my private jet ASAP."

"This way, Signora." One of the flight attendants helped Sami to the window seat in the coach section at the rear of the plane. With so much commotion, Ric was awake. On the flight over, nothing had seemed to faze him, but he was a different child right now and growing fussier by the minute.

As soon as she was settled, she picked him up out of his carrycot and held him close while she patted his back.

"We're going home, sweetheart." She'd cried so many tears, she thought she'd be dry by now. But the baby's tears started hers up all over again.

The plane filled fast. Every seat looked taken. Pat must have pulled a few strings to get Sami on this flight. She couldn't credit that they were really leaving. She felt as if her heart was being torn out of her body.

Knowing Ric, she knew she'd see him again, of course, but he'd probably be a married man when he could find the time to fly to Reno. She had no doubts he'd work out all the complications with Eliana and her father to preserve his family's honor, but nothing between Sami and Ric would ever be the same again.

Visions of their week together played through her mind like a movie, torturing her to death. The final blow came when the Fasten Seatbelts light went on. This was it.

She had to put the baby back in his cot and fasten the straps. He didn't like it at all. She pulled a bottle out of the diaper bag. Once she was strapped in, she held it to his mouth so he'd drink, but he wasn't interested and fought her.

She gave up. Once in the air, she'd be able to hold him and get him to settle down. She let his fingers curl around hers, hoping the contact would keep him preoccupied. The male passenger in army fatigues seated next to the baby smiled at her. "Hi. I'm Gary."

A real live hero from the military. He looked so totally American with his butch cut, she couldn't help but smile back. "I'm Sami. This is my son, Ric."

"He's awfully cute."

"Thanks, but he'd be a lot cuter if he weren't so upset."

Whatever the soldier said back was lost to her because she noticed a couple of Italian men in nondescript suits who didn't look like passengers walking down the aisle toward her. They were scanning the packed plane.

As they drew closer, Sami recognized one of them and gave a little gasp of shock. *Ric's bodyguards*. Her heartbeat took off at a breathtaking pace.

The men reached her row in a hurry. "Signorina Argyle? There was an irregularity with your passport before you boarded the plane. You will have to come with us please on orders of the Chief of Police." Chief Coretti was involved?

The soldier's eyes widened before he got to his feet and stepped out in the aisle to make room. One of the bodyguards took the diaper bag while the other picked up the carrycot holding her baby.

"Good luck," the soldier said as she stepped past him.

She was in too much shock to answer him, because by now another man stood behind the security men. The glint of glittering eyes black as jet was unmistakable.

"Ric!"

He must have noticed her legs start to buckle. The next thing she knew he crushed her in his strong arms. "Hold on to me, darling. Keep holding on and never let go."

"Tell me what this means," she half moaned.

Ric buried his face in her hair. "It means I'm free to ask you to marry me. If you don't say yes this instant, you're in a lifetime and beyond of trouble."

Sami didn't even take an instant before she found his

mouth to give him her answer. After having to hold back for so long, her hunger for him had taken over.

The passengers began clapping. She heard a few wolf whistles. In the background above the din she could hear their son wailing loudly enough to wake the dead, but for once she had to attend to her own needs first.

"I love you, Enrico Alberto Degenoli the thirteenth, but you've always known that."

"Sami, Sami. *Tesora mia.* I adore you."

She heard throats being cleared.

"Excellency," one of his bodyguards whispered. "We need to exit the plane so it can take off."

Sami giggled for happiness. "I'm afraid it's harder for you to get rid of your title than you thought."

"As long as it haunts everyone else, that's all that matters. Give me your mouth one more time."

Three days later she walked down the aisle of the church in Paphos with her new husband, beaming at the small crowd of beloved faces of friends and family members on both sides who'd come to see them married. Their baby rested against Pat's shoulder. When Sami looked at her sister, they had one of those communication moments.

They were both remembering Pat's warning over the phone. *You might be walking into something you wish you could have avoided. Not all people are as nice and good as you are, Sami. I don't want to see you hurt.* Was it only ten days ago?

Pat blew her a kiss. It said, *You were right to look for*

Ric's grandfather. You were on the path to your destiny.
Sami flashed her a brilliant smile.

The doors at the back of the church opened to the sunlight. What a glorious wedding day! She looked at the handsome man she'd just pledged her life to. Sami was so in love with him she couldn't contain it. "Oh, Ric—"

"I know," he said, reading her mind. "We've got to get each other to ourselves quick."

"Just a few more pictures, then we'll kiss the baby and go."

Everyone followed them outside. So many hugs and kisses, but it was clear Ric had trouble letting go of their son. Sami could be jealous, but she wasn't.

Finally they climbed in the back of the car and Vito drove them to the harbor where the cabin cruiser was waiting. As he helped them get on board, he hugged her, then his brother. Sami heard him say, "I've talked it over with Donata. She's excited to move here with everyone."

Ric gave him a bear hug back.

When they moved below to the galley, she caught his face in her hands. "What was that all about?"

"I'll tell you later. First, I need to get you out of your wedding dress. You looked like a golden-and-white angel in there today, Sami." He kissed her pliant mouth. "But will you forgive me if I confess I've been waiting to take this off you since the second I saw you in it?"

She gave him a playful smile. "I have a confession of my own to make. For eleven endless months I've longed to lie in the arms of the man who held me in the avalanche. All we had was each other and very little air to breathe. I want to re-create that time over and over again, forever."

His eyes burned like black fire, filling her with longing as he carried her to the bed. She embraced him with a love she no longer had to hide.

They lost track of time in their desire to give each other pleasure. Her unseen lover was now her husband, a man whose lovemaking brought her the most ineffable joy. Hours later they surfaced to discover it was night.

She half lay on top of him. Sami rubbed the side of his jaw with her cheek. "Hmm. I feel a little stubble. Do you know I love every single thing about you whether we're in the dark or the light?"

His deep chuckle thrilled her. "It's still not as dark in here as it was that day. I can see enough of you to want you all over again. My appetite for you is indecent."

"Then we were made for each other," she cried.

"Tell me something," he whispered, kissing a favorite spot. "Was that soldier coming on to you?"

She lifted her head. "What soldier? Oh—the one on the plane?"

"Do you know another?"

"No," She laughed because he sounded so possessive. "He thought Ric was adorable and said so."

"Then I guess I forgive him."

"Darling." She kissed him hungrily. "Now tell me about Vito's plans."

He rolled her over to look into her eyes. "With all the money assets including the palazzo and Claudia's villa turned over to Eliana's father, the debt my father accrued is paid up in full."

"I can't believe it took all that!"

"My father's vice was his own undoing, but I don't want to talk about him. The best news is, Vito has agreed to go into business with me and run a new shipping line with the assets from Mother's legacy."

She covered his face with kisses. "I know how much it means for you to be close to him."

"I believe you do. It'll be fun to see if we can build a new Degenoli empire with our own hard work, shoulder to shoulder. Both my siblings are going to buy villas here on Paphos so we can all live together."

"It's perfect, except for one thing. You haven't told me how things went with Eliana."

"That's because her father wouldn't allow me to go near her. After our business meeting concluded, he told me she was spending time at Prince Rudolfo's winter palace in Torino while she recovered."

"That's awful."

"I don't think so. She couldn't handle my having a son, and I don't blame her. Rudolfo's her type and eligible. I think they could even have a good marriage because she'll be marrying a prince. That's much better than a count."

"*Ric—*" She buried her face in his neck.

"But I don't want to think about any of that again. The only thing that matters is you. You came to Italy as I'd hoped you would, bringing me a Christmas gift that's brought me joy beyond measure. I think I willed you here."

Her breath caught. "I'm positive you did. I felt a force stronger than my own will. Ric and I need you desperately."

"Then prove it to me again, Sami. I couldn't live without you now."

Neither could she without him.

Neither could she.

* * * * *

COMING NEXT MONTH from Harlequin® Romance
AVAILABLE NOVEMBER 27, 2012

#4351 SINGLE DAD'S HOLIDAY WEDDING
Rocky Mountain Brides
Patricia Thayer
Jace is going to prove to new boss Lori who's the real boss. Is this the season for second chances?

#4352 THE SECRET THAT CHANGED EVERYTHING
The Larkville Legacy
Lucy Gordon
Charlotte and Lucio share one intensely passionate night together—a night that will affect them more than they could possibly imagine...

#4353 MISTLETOE KISSES WITH THE BILLIONAIRE
Holiday Miracles
Shirley Jump
Back in her small hometown for Christmas, can Grace find happiness the second time around with her ex-boyfriend JC?

#4354 HER OUTBACK RESCUER
Journey Through the Outback
Marion Lennox
For billionaire Hugo, ex-ballerina Amy threatens to derail his icy cool. But with no time for distractions, will he succumb to her charms?

#4355 BABY UNDER THE CHRISTMAS TREE
Teresa Carpenter
When Max's ex abandons their son, Elle steps in to help. This Christmas, the best gift of all is family!

#4356 THE NANNY WHO SAVED CHRISTMAS
Michelle Douglas
This Christmas, nanny Nicola is determined to make a difference. Cade and his little daughters are the perfect place to start...

You can find more information on upcoming Harlequin® titles, free excerpts and more at www.Harlequin.com.

HRCNM1112

REQUEST YOUR FREE BOOKS!
2 FREE NOVELS PLUS 2 FREE GIFTS!

Harlequin®

Romance

From the Heart, For the Heart

YES! Please send me 2 FREE Harlequin® Romance novels and my 2 FREE gifts (gifts are worth about $10). After receiving them, if I don't wish to receive any more books, I can return the shipping statement marked "cancel". If I don't cancel, I will receive 6 brand-new novels every month and be billed just $4.09 per book in the U.S. or $4.49 per book in Canada. That's a savings of at least 14% off the cover price! It's quite a bargain! Shipping and handling is just 50¢ per book in the U.S. and 75¢ per book in Canada.* I understand that accepting the 2 free books and gifts places me under no obligation to buy anything. I can always return a shipment and cancel at any time. Even if I never buy another book, the two free books and gifts are mine to keep forever.

116/316 HDN FESE

Name _____ (PLEASE PRINT)

Address _____ Apt. #

City _____ State/Prov. _____ Zip/Postal Code

Signature (if under 18, a parent or guardian must sign)

Mail to the **Reader Service:**
IN U.S.A.: P.O. Box 1867, Buffalo, NY 14240-1867
IN CANADA: P.O. Box 609, Fort Erie, Ontario L2A 5X3

Not valid for current subscribers to Harlequin Romance books.

**Are you a subscriber to Harlequin Romance books
and want to receive the larger-print edition?
Call 1-800-873-8635 or visit www.ReaderService.com.**

* Terms and prices subject to change without notice. Prices do not include applicable taxes. Sales tax applicable in N.Y. Canadian residents will be charged applicable taxes. Offer not valid in Quebec. This offer is limited to one order per household. All orders subject to credit approval. Credit or debit balances in a customer's account(s) may be offset by any other outstanding balance owed by or to the customer. Please allow 4 to 6 weeks for delivery. Offer available while quantities last.

Your Privacy—The Reader Service is committed to protecting your privacy. Our Privacy Policy is available online at www.ReaderService.com or upon request from the Reader Service.

We make a portion of our mailing list available to reputable third parties that offer products we believe may interest you. If you prefer that we not exchange your name with third parties, or if you wish to clarify or modify your communication preferences, please visit us at www.ReaderService.com/consumerchoice or write to us at Reader Service Preference Service, P.O. Box 9062, Buffalo, NY 14269. Include your complete name and address.

HRL1B

* * *

"I HAVE also spoken to my parents."

"They've heard?"

"They were the ones who alerted me!" Alex said. "We have aides who monitor the press and the news constantly." Did she not understand he had been up all night dealing with this? "I am waiting for the palace to ring—to see how we will respond."

She couldn't think, her head was spinning in so many directions and Alex's presence wasn't exactly calming— not just his tension, not just the impossible situation, but the sight of him in her kitchen, the memory of his kiss. That alone would have kept her thoughts occupied for days on end, but to have to deal with all this, too…. And now the doorbell was ringing. He followed her as she went to hit the display button.

"It's my dad." She was actually a bit relieved to see him. "He'll know what to do, how to handle—"

"I thought you hated scandal," Alex interrupted.

"We'll just say—"

"I don't think you understand." Again he interrupted her and there was no trace of the man she had met yesterday; instead she faced not the man but the might of

Crown Prince Alessandro Santina. "There is no question that you will go through with this."

"You can't force me." She gave a nervous laugh. "We both know that yesterday was a mistake." She could hear the doorbell ringing. She went to press the intercom but his hand halted her, caught her by the wrist. She shot him the same look she had yesterday, the one that should warn him away, except this morning it did not work.

"You agreed to this, Allegra, the money is sitting in your account." He looked down at the paper. "Of course, we could tell the truth…" He gave a dismissive shrug. "I'm sure they have photos of later."

"It was just a kiss…."

"An expensive kiss," Alex said. "I wonder what the papers would make of it if they found out I bought your services yesterday."

"You wouldn't." She could see it now, could see the horrific headlines—she, Allegra, in the spotlight, but for shameful reasons.

"Oh, Allegra," he said softly but without endearment. "Absolutely I would. It's far too late to change your mind."

* * *

Pick up PLAYING THE ROYAL GAME by Carol Marinelli on November 13, 2012, from Harlequin® Presents®.

HARLEQUIN *Presents*

When legacy commands, these Greek royals must obey!

Discover a page-turning new Harlequin Presents®
duet from *USA TODAY* bestselling author

Maisey Yates

A ROYAL WORLD APART

Desperate to escape an arranged marriage, Princess
Evangelina has tried every trick in her little black book
to dodge her security guards. But where everyone else
has failed, will her new bodyguard bend her to his
will…and steal her heart?

Available November 13, 2012.

AT HIS MAJESTY'S REQUEST

Prince Stavros Drakos rules his country like his
business—with a will of iron! And when duty demands
an heir, this resolute bachelor will turn his sole
focus to the task….

But will he finally have met his match in a world-
renowned matchmaker?

Coming December 18, 2012,
wherever books are sold.

HARLEQUIN® *Desire*

ALWAYS POWERFUL, PASSIONATE AND PROVOCATIVE.

**A brand-new Westmoreland novel
from *New York Times* bestselling author**

BRENDA JACKSON

Riley Westmoreland never mixes business with pleasure—until he meets his company's gorgeous new party planner. But when he gets Alpha Blake into bed, he realizes one night will never be enough. That's when her past threatens to end their affair. So Riley does what any Westmoreland male would do…he lets the fun begin.

ONE WINTER'S NIGHT

"Jackson's characters are…hot enough to burn the pages."
—*RT Book Reviews* on *Westmoreland's Way*

Available from Harlequin® Desire December 2012!